Jessica

ALL FOR FAMILY

A SAFE HAVEN REDISCOVERY NOVEL

LYNN BOIRE

*My precious &
loving family,*

Lynn

Cover design by Steven Novak

ISBN eBook: 978-1777-1458-0-4
ISBN Print: 978-1777-1458-1-1

CONTENTS

PRAISE FOR LYNN BOIRE

All for Love

"It's what many of us have feared....the time climate change becomes a reality. *All for Love* is about a family enduring all the trials, tribulations, and uncertainty they face, trying to find a new normal in the midst of chaos. Riveting!" ~ *Dave*

"*All for Love* opens a readers' eyes to how easily the idea of security can shift. Prepare yourself for a thought provoking tale." ~ *Suki Lang*

All for Family

"Enjoyed this one tremendously!" ~ *Darlene Y.*

"I really enjoyed the snappy dialogue. Perceptive glimpses into an Intention Living lifestyle opened my thoughts on this way of life." ~ *Karen G.*

All for Peace

"A refreshing novel that shows no one is perfect, but with love and honesty, relationships can work. Loved it." ~ *B Johnson*

"It was hard to put the novel down, the intriguing plot of romance, illusions, and murder kept me engaged until the end." ~ *A. Evans*

CHAPTER 1 - THE TAYLORS

Anna Taylor continued waving to her family—and her sister's—until both moving trucks disappeared from sight. Whew! Saying goodbye was more difficult than she imagined. However, realizing that her loved ones would be safe while she fulfilled her commitment lifted a burden from her shoulders. Wiping the moisture from her eyes, she felt proud that she hadn't broken down and cried. It wasn't sadness that occupied her heart; it was a relief.

Taking several deep breaths as she gathered her thoughts, Anna surveyed her home. Things were changing quickly, and she had no time to waste. Within three days of Matt accepting her decision to remain in Olympia, he and their children were gone, along with Kari and her husband and son.

Now, she could concentrate on getting her house in order before attacking the challenge she'd undertaken— prepare her hospital to handle outbreaks of infectious diseases.

Anna looked at the pile of construction debris beside

her home. With her carpenter brother-in-law gone, she'd have to depend on one of his associates for assistance.

She picked her way through the chaos to the side door that accessed the recent one-bedroom suite in her split-level home. The freshly painted walls and recently installed flooring gave a new-home smell. This smaller space would suit her just fine.

Anna pulled a scrunchie from her pocket and organized her hair into a loose ponytail. Taking another deep breath, she squared her shoulders. This packing wouldn't get done on its own.

Grabbing two empty boxes, she climbed the stairs to the main level and began packing her kitchen first. She'd transfer the essentials downstairs and donate the rest to a food bank.

She hoped it wouldn't take long to have that accomplished and the space leased out. A family should quickly snap up a three-bedroom home with a yard. She'd already contacted a rental agency and advised them of the type of occupants she had in mind. She'd let it go for a reasonable rate to a responsible family, as long as they looked after the yard and home maintenance. Anna didn't have the time to mow lawns or maintain the garden beds. What would happen after that was too far into the future for her to worry about right now.

Starting in the spice and pantry section, Anna gritted her teeth and reminded herself to be spartan. Taking only the necessities she'd use to make meals for herself, she quickly filled the boxes and brought them downstairs to unload. The next trip involved emptying the refrigerator and freezer.

When twilight came, she poured herself a glass of wine, collapsed onto her recliner, and raised the footrest to ease her lower back. She sighed with satisfaction. What a day. Whenever she started a project, she found it difficult to stop before completion. Compiling her to-do list, she included making signs for anything to be put in a storage facility. She'd keep her collection of sentimental items downstairs and hope their memories would warm her on the many lonely nights to come.

The phone rang, and Anna smiled as she recognized the number. "What? Miss me already?"

"Yes, I was. I wondered if you'd stopped and had dinner yet? Knowing you, you've been packing and organizing since we left."

"I'm relaxing in my chair with a glass of wine right now. Where are you?"

"We just checked in at Kingfisher Resort again. It's familiar for the kids, and we've had a long, emotional day. You realize you can change your mind anytime and join us."

"Yes, my love, I do. Please don't worry about this decision. It feels right for me, but I'm not too proud to admit if that changes. I'm looking forward to the challenge. It's a real weight off my shoulders to have the anxiety of the family's health gone. I'm certain you'll look after Jed and Lisa and the rest of the crew while I deal with this."

"Of course. Kari's having doubts about leaving you behind."

"I'll call her tomorrow and let her know how thankful I am that she's added two kids to her role as a mother while I'm down here. I couldn't have done this without all of your support."

"It's been a team effort. I'm sure once we get organized in our new home, it will sink in for the children more. It's an adventure right now. I'm planning the old "idle hands" approach. They won't have time to regret the move as much if they're actively helping me get Safe Haven ready for the new residents coming in. It will give them lots to talk to you about during your FaceTime visits."

"That's true. Aren't you expecting the new arrivals soon?"

"Yes, the Camerons will arrive by late May, then the Zanettis by mid-June. They're waiting for their house sale to go through and for their daughter to finish her exams."

"Good, I'm sure Lisa will be happy to have another girl to hang around with, even if Chloe's a few years older. Moving up the timeline meant we didn't have as much time to get the kids ready for the adjustment. I hope they're going to be okay."

"That's true, but Kari's been great about staying close to Lisa. The boys won't be a problem. They're excited about the whole thing. Don't worry. We'll all manage." Matt's voice deepened with conviction. "We've got this, sweetheart."

"I know. Once you get the internet set up, we'll set up a video chat before I start with orientation. It's going to be an extremely hectic first week. Starting this coming Monday, I'm attending a FEMA web seminar so that I understand what I'll be responsible for." Anna paused and sipped her wine, sharing information she had held back for lack of personal discussion time.

"The following week, I'm scheduled to meet with the Duty Officer for Tacoma General Hospital, who'll give me an overview of the healthcare coalition in the Puget Sound region." Anna's spirits perked up as she pondered all the avenues she'd be exploring to give her hospital the tools needed for the current outbreak of Legionnaire's.

"Sounds like you've got the challenges you've always wanted to tackle all lined up and waiting." Anna could tell Matt was tempering his concern with her enthusiasm to be part of the solution. "But I can't see how this will help your hospital right away. I thought you needed to be on-site, directing things."

"I'll be doing both. The Zoom webinars are held from 8 until ii a.m., followed by an hour of questions and input from different areas. After lunch, I'll head to the hospital and deal with whatever needs attention." Anna kept her tone light and eager, trying to reassure her husband she was still confident of her decision.

"Just don't wear yourself down, Anna. Take time to rest between shifts. It's important not to get stressed. You won't be helping anyone if your immune system weakens and you get sick too."

"I've already given myself that lecture. I promised you I'd be careful, and I will be. Let's arrange for Sunday night chats for sure, and I'll try and get another one in during the week once things slow down. I'm heading for a hot bath and will turn in early tonight. Give my love to the kids and Kari."

"Done. Remember, I love you, sweetheart."

Anna clicked off her phone, thinking about the journey ahead, and smiled in anticipation. Call her crazy, but she couldn't wait to join the various agencies involved with the HERT—the Hospital Emergency Response Team.

As Anna adjusted her heavy satchel on her shoulder and exited the elevator, she heard a familiar voice call out.

"Anna!" Her supervisor, Leanne, crooked a finger for Anna to follow her down the hall to her office.

"I see you have material to read. Overwhelmed yet?"

"Almost. There *is* an awful lot of information to take in. I've never delved into the administration side of operating a hospital before. But it's fascinating, especially when it comes to coordinating supplies and responses."

"I imagined you might enjoy the challenge. It's not for everyone. You have to be the type who likes to look ahead and anticipate both the challenge and the response. I'm glad you've joined us. It was time for us to train or hire ourselves a duty officer."

"I have to admit feeling not very helpful right now. Is there something you'd like me to focus on while I learn the layout?"

"Hire an assistant. You'll need one to handle the research and detail work, so you're free to decide if our current problem gets out of control. Your initial idea to isolate a space with outside ventilation separate from the rest of the hospital was fantastic. The contractors tore down the wall between the staff and storage rooms to create six intensive care units for contagious patients. They're working double shifts, and the plumbing, oxygen, and water, as well as electrical for computerized equipment, is underway already. We'll soon be treating patients there."

"Great. Where will the staff and storage rooms be relocated to?"

"For now, they'll go downstairs in two of the instructional rooms we reserve for medical students taking their residency here. It's the best short-term solution. We'll figure out an alternative down the road."

"Smart thinking. For an assistant, do you have anyone in mind? Should I transfer someone from within or look externally?"

"That's up to you. I trust your judgment. You'll need to consider your assistant's family situation and whether they can handle high-stress situations. For instance, if your applicant has small children at home, it may limit available work hours unless they have a good support system. Their temperament also will indicate whether they can think outside the box and find solutions to time-sensitive situations. And of course, compatibility and trust." Leanne grinned at Anna and gave her a thumbs-up. "Welcome to HERT."

Anna returned the gesture and thanked her. "Where's my office? I'll need somewhere to call home."

"Third floor in the rehab ward. It's pretty quiet up there, and I've commandeered an office set up for you at the end of the hall. If you need anything else, let me know. How about we meet tomorrow after work and discuss what you've learned so far?"

"Sounds great. Say 5:30? My office or yours? Or shall we meet for dinner while we chat?"

"Let's do the first one off-site. I'm craving Italian at Romeo's."

"Perfect. I'll meet you there. Thanks, Leanne."

Leanne nodded. "I hope you still are thanking me a month from now." She laughed as she walked toward her office.

Anna returned to the elevator and pressed the button for the third floor, thinking about Leanne's parting comment. Already this job looked to be more than just organizing staff and supplies for the current crisis. Maybe it was the carrot to the posting of Duty Officer. The title sounded so monotonous, yet the complicated assignment was anything but.

Reading the prerequisite manual regarding the Federal agencies responsible for managing catastrophes, Anna soon realized how uninformed she was about coordinating aid for natural disasters and infectious diseases. After joining the FEMA orientation meeting on Monday, she learned about the various alerts and the communications necessary to facilitate assistance between healthcare facilities. Any delay in food and medical supply transportation, or surge in medical staff needs, could result in disastrous consequences.

Anna's head was spinning. Not that she needed to know all the ins and outs, but she had to be aware of them. The Zoom meetings had also touched on the need for each hospital to be self-sufficient for a minimum of ninety-six hours for oxygen, food, water, electricity, and fuel for generators. The emergency management program was a place she'd be referring to often.

This network was where she'd obtain all necessary information. Every integrated region in every state would become invaluable for relocating the most vulnerable during a red alert. It was also the source that they would turn to in case of a shortage of medical staff or supplies. Thank God she planned and videotaped the session so that she could review the subjects again. Reading manuals was one thing, but the interactions and experiences that the participants shared made the situations more real and urgent.

Anna was warmly greeted on the third floor and congratulated on her new assignment. She'd worked in this ward for a few years as a post-op and rehab nurse, so it felt good to have her office near people she could depend on. Dashing to the end of the hall, she unlocked the door to Room 312 and perused her new domain.

The decision to open a new position must have resulted in an influx of money. On the far side, Leanne had placed a new desk and chair perpendicular to the large window overlooking the parking lot, and in the distance, the waters of Puget Sound. Two other chairs were positioned on the other side of her desk. It looked like Leanne was expecting her to be busy. A beige room divider separated the office, with another smaller desk, phone, computer, and chair ready to occupy. A locking file cabinet and an accompanying shelving unit were waiting for attention.

Anna removed her jacket, hung it on the umbrella tree, and then plopped her briefcase on her desk. She stood near the window for a minute, enjoying the feeling of accomplishment. Hard to believe she had her own office. Anna sat in her chair, adjusting the seat and forearm height. She'd be devoting a lot of time here, and ergonomics would make the difference in the long hours she was sure she'd be keeping. Opening the drawers, Anna found a note and the key to the filing cabinet where a new laptop was preprogrammed for her use. All interfaces would need new passwords, and she was instructed to call Leanne when she was ready to boot up.

Anna took out two 4x6 framed photos of her family, taken on their last trip together to Bella Coola. A spontaneous picture of the family in the snow beside their ATVs, drinking cups of hot chocolate. The sparkle in their eyes said it all. The other was a silhouette of Matt and Anna holding hands, walking along the shoreline. Kari had snapped the photo one evening at their beach house, and it reminded Anna of the rejuvenation they enjoyed last summer.

A knock at the door and Mia entered the office with two mugs of coffee in her hand.

"Congratulations, Anna! I'm so glad they've put you up here with us. I hope you'll join us anytime you want in the lunchroom. If there's anything you need help with, just say so. You have friends here. We'd be happy to help."

"Thanks, Mia. I could use a caffeine kick right now— you must have read my mind. There's so much to do. Have a seat if you've got a minute." Anna took a sip of the potent brew while Mia made herself comfortable. "For the foreseeable future, it looks like my nose will be stuck in manuals or on a computer. I've got a lot to learn. I may have to get my own Keurig to keep me going." Anna ruefully chuckled. "Anything new on this ward that I should know? Any signs of infection popping up? I've been catching up with things at home before starting this job, so I'm a bit behind. Have you seen Gina or heard anything on her progress?"

"She's recuperating, but it's slow. Someone usually texts her during the day and lets the rest of us know. Gina's still in isolation but should be out in a few more days once they're sure the bug's out of her system. Then she'll enter a regular ward until the doctors declare her strong enough to return home."

"Ron calls me every few days. He was so worried about her, but she's so stubborn, it was hard to get her to the emergency ward. Apparently, that won't be a problem anymore. Gina's promised her family she'll listen to them and not be so hesitant about calling an ambulance." Anna shrugged her shoulders, uncertain whether Gina could keep that promise.

"I know. It's hard for us healthcare workers. We don't want to cause a fuss over potentially nothing, which is admirable, but sometimes it's the wrong thing to do. We're a stubborn bunch."

"It's a lesson for all of us." Anna frowned as she remembered her friend's brush with acute pneumonia from Legionnaire's.

Anna tried to force Gina to come to the hospital, but she refused until it was almost too late. When Gina took a turn for the worse, it not only frightened her family but had triggered an ultimatum from Matt. Now her family was gone. Anna blew out a sigh as she thought of what lay ahead.

"I'd better get moving and call Leanne so I can get my computer running and check the stats in the emergency ward. Thanks for the coffee, Mia. We'll do lunch one day."

"You bet. Don't be a stranger. Call if you need any help." Mia left the office, waving goodbye.

SEVERAL HOURS LATER, Anna pushed her chair away and arched her spine, rolling her shoulders to loosen the tension. She rubbed her eyelids tenderly, trying to clear the gritty feeling. Opening her purse, Anna retrieved her saline drops and applied several to each eye, blinking furiously to stop tears from flowing.

Enough. Anna looked outside into the night sky and remembered her promise to Matt. Guess she already blew it today. The meeting with Leanne was lengthy. There were so many databases Anna had access to that she wasn't sure where to start. Thank goodness Leanne had anticipated her needs. They made a synergistic team.

Leanne entered Anna's office and opened a Word document, and bookmarked it for easy access. "I figured the scope of this project might overwhelm you at first, so I created a simplified document with links ready for you to study. It's a chart that outlines each agency involved in emergency preparedness, both federally and at the state level." See here? This network is where it starts. Each agency has a guideline and mandate to follow. I've listed the items that pertain to the healthcare policies, so you can follow the branches to get the information you need. Right now, we're focused on Legionnaire's disease. Your goal is to assess our resource availability and what we need to have in place so we'll be able to maintain a continuity of operations."

"Leanne, I'm beginning to doubt that you have the right person for this. It's mind-boggling." Anna dropped her head in her hands on the desk as the frustration mounted, then looked up into Leanne's eyes. "There's so much to absorb. How will I get this job completed within the two months Matt and I agreed upon? I'm just not sure how quickly I'll pick this up. There's so much to learn." Anna returned to her laptop to look at the newly installed programs. A small groan escaped Anna as she realized the scope of her project.

"Everything seems overwhelming the first few days you start a new job. Don't forget most of this has been organized in other regions, and you only need to follow their lead. Take a deep breath, Anna. It's not as bad as it looks right now. We have a great working relationship with Tacoma General. After you look over the statistics for the past week, I want you to arrange a meeting with Fiona Halvorsen over there." Leanne sat opposite Anna and leaned forward. "C'mon, put a smile on your face and jump in like you usually do."

Anna looked up from her laptop and took a deep breath. "You're right. It's not like I have a family to run home to. With them safe in Bella Coola, I can work evenings and weekends if I need to."

"You'll find a way." Leanne stood up and moved towards the door. "You'll like Fiona. Once you see how their hospital is faring with their caseload, you'll see how you can improve ours. It isn't impossible. She is part of the Puget Sound Coalition. We help each other out as much as possible. Fiona knows her stuff and can probably give you lots of good pointers." Leanne reached over and squeezed her shoulder. "One step at a time, girl. You're not alone. I've seen you handle challenges before, and I know you can manage this too. I texted Fiona this morning, asking her to be available for your cries for help this week."

"Oh, that sounds encouraging." Anna sighed. "I'm sure that's the last thing she wants to do is babysit a newbie in our emergency response team."

"Don't worry, Fiona's only been at her job two or three years herself. She remembers how bewildered she felt. I'm sure she'll be generous with her advice and her contacts at the supply chains we all use."

"Ok. I'll set up a meeting for tomorrow afternoon. Meanwhile, I think I'd better pull up some stats and start figuring out where we're sitting. Maybe when we get together tomorrow for dinner, I'll have some intelligent news to deliver."

FIONA WAS as accommodating as Leanne predicted. To save time, they arranged a Zoom meeting. Fiona showed Anna a model of the centralized warehouse where consultants streamlined the procurement process. Seldom were hospitals shorted on pharmaceuticals. The supply chain was well established, as was the food chain.

"The one area I'm most concerned with is the inventory each hospital has for personal protective gear. It surprised me when I ordered the N95 masks for infectious disease protection. I only received half of what I ordered, and the other half is back-ordered, with no timeline for delivery."

"That's crazy. You'd think the warehouse would stockpile those items after the last scare we had with the SARS epidemic." The surprise and disappointment in Anna's voice came across strong and clear.

"That was over ten years ago, and I suspect the warehouse became complacent and slowly let it dwindle. Now they're trying to outsource a new supply chain, but that takes time to set up."

"Do you know what's the current case numbers are in that category in our area?" Anna asked.

"Yes. I'll walk you through the process to get the information. Log onto HERT. Once you're in, go to the coded alert system for Puget Sound. Let me know when you get there."

Anna could hear Fiona tapping her keyboard, obviously searching for more information as Anna navigated the site. "Got it. I see it."

"Then you see how it branches out to get more detailed information? Bypass the stat reports for now and go straight to the incident reports."

"I see the list of hospitals and the cases in each one. Hmm. It's not as bad as I thought it might be."

"We were lucky to have caught the outbreak early. After the coalition received help from FEMA, they broadcast the information through television, radio podcasts, and cell phone alerts. It's made a world of difference. The problem we need to concentrate on now is awareness."

"Of what?"

"Of how unprepared we are. That's why management hired you. FEMA has great control of the communication systems, but they have fallen behind with demand forecasting and procurement. Locally, we've fallen behind in our approach to the distribution network and how we would help each area in an emergency. We're already at a staff shortage level since our population has jumped. So, what happens when we need extra help? Where do we go?" Fiona lifted an eyebrow, looking for Anna's input.

"I honestly don't know, and that's frightening. So many people don't see the real problem with the climate refugees from the south. The problems aren't with the people themselves, but with the overload they cause in the system. Believe it or not, my family got caught in a riot, with shots fired last summer. Everyone felt the panic, even the protestors."

"Leanne told me about that and sent me a video clip. You were chosen because you didn't fly off the handle. We need a cool head to make decisions, and you've earned respect within the hospital. You'll need to set up a program for all levels of staff to enroll to upgrade their skills in infectious disease control. That was one of the first programs I set up at my facility. Every three years, everyone has to take a refresher course to reinforce their skills to reduce cross-contamination. And an update on identifying the most recent potentially infectious diseases must be part of the plan."

"So, I'm hoping you still have all your notes?" Anna was again feeling overwhelmed.

"Sure do. Sharing information is part of the mandate of a centralized coalition for HERT in the state of Washington. Any healthcare facility that needs help or has run a successful program is encouraged to share information. In the long run, the more facilities that are prepared, the better off we'll be."

"I hear you. Please send what you have over to me as soon as you can. I need to have a chat with Leanne too. I have a feeling Legionnaire's was only the hook to get me in here. I'm not sure I'm ready for the long-term commitment you're suggesting I need to have."

"Good idea. You should know what you've got yourself into. Just know I've worked interagency with your boss, and she's a brilliant chess player. She's always looking two or three steps ahead. If Leanne thinks you're the one to bring your hospital up to par, you should be proud."

"Thanks, Fiona. I'll wait for your info and call you back when I've digested it. Thank God for video conferencing. It's sure saved me a lot of precious time. Compared to reading manuals, it's so much easier to get the gist of how things work."

"Ditto. Chat soon. By the end of the day, all the information should be in your in-box." Fiona winked. "Smile, Anna. You can do this. Just holler if you need more help."

"Thanks for your vote of confidence. I'm sure you'll hear from me more often than your family does, at least for the first few weeks."

"Not a problem." Fiona sent an emoticon waving goodbye and closed the session.

THE FIRST FEW weeks were the hardest, as Anna learned what to expect in her new position. At first, she had appreciated the solitude to concentrate on research for the Hospital Emergency Response Team. Anna would come home late, order food, heat a frozen entrée, then dig into the paperwork for another few hours. Now that she felt she understood the processes to access help better, she put her manual together for the various departments in her hospital. Fiona's contribution of training manuals to start a mandated system for emergency safety protocol saved Anna weeks of work. But now, as things leveled off, Anna noticed that although the stress was reducing, it also allowed an emptiness to surface.

Watching the excited family move in upstairs was heart-warming. The two boys eagerly explored the backyard, climbing the rungs in the maple tree to Jed's old tree-fort. The rental agency had sent Anna a short list of four families. The Lees were the second family she had interviewed, and Anna immediately felt a connection with them. She emailed Ray and asked him to send one of his previous crew members to do some repairs for her.

When Darren arrived, Anna had him put steel-clad doors on either side of the shared laundry room so that they'd all feel confident that privacy would be assured. Then she had Darren check out the tree-fort and rungs, replacing anything that was deteriorating. Anna pulled out the soccer net and balls left behind in the storage shed, so the enthusiastic boys would enjoy the backyard as much as her children had. It would be good to hear the laughter once more, even if it did trigger a longing to be with her family again.

Their last video call had lasted over an hour, with Lisa and Jed recounting their ATV adventures around the retreat. Matt and Kari had registered the kids in Bella Coola for school a week after they arrived. From what Anna could glean, the boys found it easier to take the bus to the high school and meet new friends than Lisa did. She was feeling shy and isolated at the middle school. Kari had stepped in and become her confidant and friend, sharing time together. Anna could see Lisa was having more trouble than her brother, so she was very thankful for her sister's presence, even if it caused a smidgen of jealousy.

Unfortunately, it was Matt that gave her the most worry. He looked fit and happy with the move, but she could tell he was getting antsy about her decision to remain behind. With his contacts and internet access, he could see the progress in the Legionnaire's outbreak. No recent episodes in the past two weeks meant that the infectious stage of the disease had passed without new cases. Only the isolated cases in the hospital remained to be cared for until they were strong enough to be released to home care.

"I saw the news report last night, Anna. This epidemic has been resolved sooner than either one of us thought it would. How's Gina doing?" Matt's eyes looked hopeful as he searched hers for the answers he wanted.

"She's doing well at home now. Gina's started minor household chores and has begun to cook again. Ron still does the clean-up after dinner, as well as laundry on the weekends, but they seemed to have found a routine that works for them." Anna wiggled her hand in front of her. "I don't know when Gina became so patient. It used to be that no one could do anything for her. She was so independent. Now, her daughter, Jan, comes almost daily and drops off homemade soups or casseroles to help out. Ron says she's doing her deep breathing exercises with the spirometer several times a day, so that should help get her lungs functioning better."

"I guess you haven't been to see her?"

"No, better safe than sorry. I use a mask religiously at the hospital, but there's no way I want to bring any bug near in her state. So, we FaceTime, which always cheers us up. Almost as much as my visits with you. I miss you and the kids. You all seem happy with life there."

"We are, for the most part. The only thing that would make it better is if you were here. I know you've appreciated the new posting you took, and it's been quite the challenge for you. Of course, you take pleasure with that sort of thing, but now that this crisis is ending, *when* are you going to give

Leanne your notice?"

"Not for a while. I'm right in the middle of setting up a program for our hospital to use if another infectious episode breaks out. With Legionnaire's, we were almost down to the last dozen cases of PPEs. That can't happen again. We didn't have the policy to track our warehouse inventory and stockpiles. I'm still networking with a coalition of other facilities to build an emergency preparedness plan. We were lucky that we only had a token outbreak."

"Look, you promised that when this was under control, you'd join us. Let someone else handle this. We need you up here."

Anna felt her heart begin to race. Her breath hitched as she tried to reassure her husband. "You don't *need* me. It wouldn't be a catastrophe if I were gone another few months. I understand that things are harder without me there, but you're not *suffering*. I'm so close to completing this program. I want to stay and do it. If I leave now, it sets the entire program back at least a month or two. And who knows if that would make a difference or not if another medical crisis arose."

"Really? Are you choosing to stay there instead of coming here? It's not only the possibility of another epidemic or the overcrowding in the hospitals that I worry about." Matt's voice had quickened and deepened. Anna could hear the frustration creeping into his voice. "What about Lisa and Jed? Our son is managing well, but Lisa's not. She's moody, and I worry that she's becoming depressed. She misses you, and I'm sure she wonders why you're still there and not here with us. Where are your priorities?"

Anna glanced down, no longer able to hide the guilt in her eyes. "I'm sorry that Lisa's having problems. I'll call Kari and see if she can spend more time with her." Anna met

Matt's stormy eyes and raised her voice. "You need to support me in this, Matt. Show the children you're proud of me, make them understand how important this is. Your continued patience and admiration for my work will encourage them to accept this. It's not forever—I've almost completed my goal."

"And what about the continued protests I see online. Do you think we don't worry about that?"

"Honestly, it's no worse now than when you left. You've been gone, what? Three months now? And sure, there are still shortages sometimes with gas or groceries, and tempers flare. The housing and healthcare problems haven't changed one bit either. But more government initiatives are being brought forward that will eventually make a difference. Trust me. If the situation becomes more dangerous, I would jump ship and join you tomorrow."

"Promise?" Matt's tone had dropped a level as anger turned to concern.

"I do." Anna projected a lilt in her voice as she cocked her head to the side. "But you'll be happy to know we have a sweet family living upstairs. Chris and Nikki Lee have two young boys, about six and eight years old. They're both teachers and so excited to get out of an apartment and into a home."

Matt's smile hadn't reached his eyes, but Anna felt that she had diffused the separation issue once again, without giving in to the guilt she felt for refusing to join her family.

"I'm glad you've found someone for our home. It makes me feel a lot better that you're not by yourself at night anymore." Matt lowered his voice, becoming as deep and earnest as his eyes. "But it doesn't change the fact that you're living in dangerous times down there, and I want you to join us as soon as you can."

"I'm trying to get to a point where someone else can take over easily. I'll do the best I can, I promise. Let's talk about our Safe Haven." Anna tried to shift gears away from herself. "Do you have any solid dates for the Armstrongs' arrival? Anyone else?"

"Yes, last week, the Cameron family arrived. The Zanettis and Armstrongs are on schedule to arrive by late June or early July."

"I'm glad to hear the Zanettis will be there soon. It will give Lisa a girl to pal around with, even if she's a little older than her. Hanging out with your aunt is one thing, but kids need kids around them. What else is new? Are Ray and Thomas getting the main lodge completed?"

"All done. The painting is completed. Now that the weather is improving and the grounds are drying up, they will work on outdoor areas next. Our workforce is expanding, and it makes the projects get completed that much faster. We've decided on three separate plots for bulk gardening, with southern exposure, which will need fencing around them."

"I remember Thomas offering to arrange a work bee to get that done. Is that still on?"

"It is. We'll be hauling in truckloads of composted dirt and seaweed once the weather gets warmer, probably early June. Then we'll have a weekend rototilling the soil. Thomas' cousins are going to come a few weeks later and help us plant root vegetables and other staples we can preserve for the winter."

"Don't forget the recreation area for the kids."

"Don't worry—with Jed and Aaron around, they won't let us forget about setting up a basketball hoop. Although I think they'll need to be satisfied with soccer this year. We just have too much to do this summer."

"You'll figure it out, sweetheart." Anna saw the strain in his eyes as he thought of the many projects ahead of him. Time to switch the subject. She lowered her voice to a purr. "You're looking good, don't forget I miss you and love you." Anna saw the twinkle come back in his eyes and his left eyebrow waggle. She felt a flush of pleasure overcome her, sending a shiver of need through her. "We'll make up for lost time soon. Hug the kids for me. I'll be there as soon as I can. Only two more months tops, then I leave. If it's not complete, it will be close enough for someone else to finish. Deal?"

"Deal. Two months max. Maybe I'll take a flight to Campbell River to meet you. We'll spend some private time together before coming back here. I need another honeymoon after all this time." Matt growled.

Anna laughed at both of his eyebrows dancing suggestively.

"I know, sweetheart. I'm looking forward to it too."

Anna closed the video chat and sat back in her chair, contemplating her next moves. As Fiona suggested, Leanne had tempted her with the challenge she undertook, but she also had other motives. Anna expected a stint of three or four months max to organize staffing and supplies during the Legionnaire's crisis. While she genuinely enjoyed testing herself, pushing herself to learn new things, she wouldn't have taken the job had she known that it could be several months before her mission was complete.

It wasn't part of the deal. Yet Leanne knew it would become a passion for Anna to find a solution to the immediate problem of not being prepared for a medical disaster. Her supervisor knew Anna liked to think and plan to avoid preventable delays or shortages, so she had appealed to her sense of responsibility.

And it had worked. Anna had expanded her knowledge base to encompass demand forecasting, distribution networking, and trace and track operations. Her warm personality attracted co-operation from the Puget Sound Coalition. She knew if something unforeseen happened tomorrow, she'd be able to reach out and get a plan in effect quickly.

Anna shut her computer down, then went to the kitchen and poured herself a glass of wine. She sat on the sofa, feet on the coffee table, as she thought about her recent challenges. Thank goodness she had hired Rachel as a research assistant. Her age almost disqualified her from the list of potential applicants. At twenty-four, Anna hadn't expected her to be as dedicated to the project and its importance as she was. But Rachel had a mind that raced ahead, anticipating answers to questions that Anna hadn't even asked. She was sharp, loyal, and ambitious, precisely what Anna was looking for in her assistant. She picked up her cell and speed-dialed her assistant.

"Hi Rachel, have you got a minute?"

"Sure, give me ten, and I'll call you back. I'm just getting out of the shower."

"Thanks. If you're not busy, pour yourself a glass of wine before returning my call."

"OK." A sliver of worry crept into Rachel's voice. "Is this good news or bad news?"

"Good. Nothing to worry about," Anna reassured. "Just needed to chat for a while."

While Anna waited for the call, she went to her bedroom and changed into lounging pajamas and slippers. The floors in the former basement were downright chilly, something she wasn't used to when living upstairs. Pouring pretzels into a bowl, she brought them into the living room and commanded Alexa to put on soft background music. Fortified, she sat and waited for Rachel.

"That was quick." Anna chuckled. "Did I pique your interest?"

"Of course, you know me. I hate to wait for information. What's up?"

"Just thinking about our progress so far. You joined me a week after I set up the office. Have you enjoyed it?"

"Yes, I have. I didn't expect to join you on webinars or Zoom meetings with other Duty Officers. It's been so challenging. Things that I always took for granted became complicated issues that had to be broken down and assessed for continued viability. I love it. This whole preparedness gig is a massive network that is totally behind the scenes. I never knew we competed with other states to get our supplies or that the federal government had that much influence in what we could or couldn't buy."

"I know. Blows your mind, doesn't it?" Anna put her phone on speaker, so she could sip her wine and be comfortable.

"It does. It reminds me of studying political science at UW. It was one of my favorite courses."

"That makes sense now—why you like working in this department."

"You do too, don't you?"

"I love a challenge, and that's how Leanne roped me in. When I got here and realized the scope of the various emergency programs, I was hooked. I wanted to decipher the maze involved in getting orders for our hospital on budget *and* on time. To ensure our procurement strategies had checks and balances, so we never ran short again."

"Leanne must be thrilled with the work you've done.

You'd never know that you were clueless just three months ago."

"Thanks. I think." Anna smiled as she paused for another sip of wine. "Only problem is, my husband and the kids are in Canada. I promised I'd follow them as soon as this outbreak was under control. Now he's calling me on it. I get it, I do, but I also hate to leave a project half-finished."

"Have you talked to Leanne? Maybe she'd let you do this remotely. There are lots of resident-based businesses around. I know of a few unit clerks that used to work in the hospital who now work from home. They access everything through a secure network and input data from the doctors and nurses onto a patient record."

"True, and it saves much-needed space on the ward too. It's a practical idea that's used more and more. The only problem is that in Bella Coola, the internet capabilities are spotty, so I doubt that would be a good fit for me. So, if you don't mind me asking, I'm wondering what your career plans are. What are your current goals?"

"Paying off my student loans is priority one. The next thing is that I don't want to be in a boring, dead-end job. I want to love what I do and excel at it, then move up to bigger and better things. I crave finding new horizons."

"You sound just like I did at your age, always looking for the next mountain to climb. But you're enjoying the field we're working in right now, aren't you? It's not monotonous, is it?"

"Love it, and it's far from dull. Why?"

"Just wondering. One thing about the HERT, it's the closest network to helping doctors and hospitals deal with immediate crises directly. But really, it's at the bottom of the network. There would be an exciting future ahead if you were interested. You could move up into the American

College and Health Care, the Domestic Preparation Office, FEMA, or the FEPA...it literally could be a lifetime career. You'd always be on your toes, on top of policy positions, anticipating, and preparing to protect all levels of the public during disasters."

"Wow. That's quite a set of possibilities."

"If you're the ambitious sort, this might be the stepping stone to move up. It doesn't happen quickly. You have to put your time in, listen to experienced people and learn. Nobody likes a hotshot, but if you're diligent and co-operative, you could go far in this field."

"Wow again. You know I work hard, and I've loved joining you and learning about the entire organization. Yes, I would be interested down the road. I'm not ready yet."

"I wasn't ready when I took this on either. However, I'm glad I did. I've made a lot of contacts and made a few friends. If I was younger and my family was still living here, I think I'd continue. Challenges like these don't come often, and it would be an opportunity to move up when a position became vacant."

"Are you trying to tell me you're quitting?" Anna heard the uncertainty in Rachel's voice.

"Soon. So, if you're interested in following in my footsteps, I'll make sure you're beside me in all my meetings so the coalition gets to know you. Then when the time's right, I'll let Leanne know I have a qualified replacement. What do you think?"

"Are you sure?" Rachel's voice became higher pitched with anticipation. "Wow. I'd love to try. It's a challenge, but it's something I think I could do well. I've got a mind for details, and I'm not afraid of long hours." Rachel giggled breathlessly, her speech becoming more animated. "Oh my gosh, I can't believe this, Anna. This opportunity is so cool."

"I'm not guaranteeing you the job. I'm saying if you're interested, and if you can commit to working co-operatively with the coalitions, then I'll let you tag along so you can learn more about it. Keep this to yourself, though. When the time comes, the decision will be up to you and Leanne. It'll be hard to leave this, but who knows the future? If things don't work out in Bella Coola, I may come back and apply for a position in Emergency Response rather than return to nursing."

"I can't stop saying, wow. I'm excited that you think I'd be a good fit for your replacement. That's quite a compliment. I'll work hard with you so that you won't have any regrets. And maybe one day, we'll work together again."

"You never know, Rachel. My wine glass is empty. Time for one more before bed. I'll see you at work tomorrow morning." Anna smiled as she disconnected, happy with Rachel's response. She felt good inside that she had taken the first step to reunite with her family.

CHAPTER 2 - THE CAMERONS

"A re you sure you're ready for this?" Nathan Cameron crept up behind his wife, winding his arms around her. "We've been apart before. We can continue to work this way."

"No thanks. This project is not the same as your other research assignments from UW, and hardly anything's been cataloged there. You'll have enough work to last you a decade. I don't want the boys to grow up away from you for months at a time. Neither do I." Brianna turned and wrapped her arms around his neck, pulling him in for a kiss.

The boys ran into the living room, hollering at each other. Imaginative and rambunctious, Tyler and Troy were like twin cyclones, creating joyful havoc wherever they played. Almost two years apart, they finished each other's sentences while driving their poor parents insane with their chatter. Getting them out of a rental townhouse in downtown Olympia and into their own home in the country would be a positive change.

"We're hungry. Can we have some cookies?"

"Indoor voices, please. Yes, but you have to have a piece of fruit first." Brianna went to the fridge and took out two apples. When they groaned, Brianna frowned. "You can't be too hungry then if you can't manage an apple first. Come back after your snack, then we'll see about the cookies."

The boys knew better than to argue with their mom over snacks. She seldom gave in. They caught the apples as she lobbed one to each of them, then tore out into the hallway to the elevator.

"I'm looking forward to the change. I didn't know Matt, but I've met Anna and Kari at the school's fundraising events. If they're ready to handle the challenge, then I feel confident that I can too. Neither one strikes me as a holy roller type, so it makes me feel more comfortable about community living. Besides, it's not a lifetime commitment. We've signed up for two years, which will fly by in no time. If we don't like it, we can find a place in town or figure something else out." Brianna reassured her husband's palpable fear of bringing his family to the boonies.

"That's very true. When I talked to Matt, that was another thing that made me sway towards joining his family at Safe Haven. Having a network of families living together will allow us to take the odd trip together. Your photography and my clinical observations on Species at Risk could be the breakthrough we need. We might even make it into the National Geographic."

"I know. I'm excited about the possibilities. We've never worked together like that. It could be an exciting experiment." Brianna's eyes sparkled in anticipation of working side by side with her husband.

Looking around at the items boxed in their living room labeled for the Salvation Army, Nathan realized how much 'stuff' they had accumulated but didn't need. As outlined in a memo from Matt, they only had a thousand square feet and a loft to live in, so they were to be as spartan as possible. They had already decided the loft would be their research area, and should their work grow to a point it needed more space, they could find somewhere in town to store the background data. Thank God, printed research textbooks were mainly a thing of the past. Those heavy tomes would have no room in their small home.

AN HOUR LATER, Brianna stepped out onto the balcony of their third-floor apartment and looked over to the play area, spotting her carrot-topped sons. They were playing on the jungle gym along with several of their friends. She blew two short whistles to gather their attention and have them return home. Rather than yelling, several of the families had arranged a series of signals to call their children home. She watched them say goodbye to their friends and run towards their complex.

"Clean up, boys. Pizza will be here in twenty minutes. It's going to be an early night for us. We have to get up very early to take our beds apart and pack our things. Aren't you excited?"

Troy shoved his brother out of the way and ran down the hall to use the washroom first.

Tyler hung back with a sad expression on his face. "I'm going to miss my friends, Mom. And my school. When are we coming back?"

"We've talked about this several times, Tyler. Maybe by the time you're ready for middle or high school, we'll return here. We'll see how much we like it up there. There are so many things you'll get to enjoy for the first time—your own yard, having animals around. Imagine learning to ride a horse or gathering fresh eggs for breakfast! We can even book time on ATVs and go exploring on trails around our new home."

"And fishing, don't forget the fishing."

Brianna smiled. Tyler knew the benefits by heart already. They'd certainly gone over them enough times. "Yes, you'll get to go river fishing with us. Once in a while, we'll go on the ocean and fish for salmon." She set paper plates, plastic cutlery, and napkins on the table for dinner.

"And we'll see seals and maybe even whales." Tyler's hazel eyes sparkled, and his voice became high-pitched as he jumped from one foot to the other. At that age, time seemed to take forever before any event happened. It finally sunk in that the long-planned trip would start in the morning.

"Yes, we will see all those things, eventually. So now, do you think it's worth going up there for a while?"

Troy joined in the discussion while Brianna scooted Tyler towards the bathroom. The access doorbell chimed, and Nathan buzzed the Domino's Pizza delivery inside their building. Nathan went to the fridge and poured milk for the boys, then took out two beers for them. Toasting each other, they enjoyed a sip before the pizza arrived at their suite's door, excited themselves with the journey ahead.

NATHAN LOADED his five-ton rental truck onto the ferry's cargo section, then went to their SUV to collect Tyler and

Troy. Yesterday, they had traveled with their father in the storage truck to one of the recommended halfway points, Mount Washington Hotel in Courtenay. The following morning, it had been Brianna's turn to entertain the boys during the four-hour road trip from the hotel to Port Hardy.

"Grab your backpacks, fellas. We're heading upstairs to our berth."

"What's a berth?" Troy inquired as he thrust his arms through the straps and shrugged them onto his back.

"It's like a hotel room but smaller. We all have bunk beds for tonight. When we get inside, I need you to help put your stuff away before exploring the ship. You remember the drill?"

"Yes, Dad. Let's go. Hurry up."

Nathan chuckled and gave Brianna a quick kiss. "See you later. Text me when you're ready to be around these two again. There's a lounge in the front of the boat. You might want to relax before joining us."

"Damn fine idea. I'll give you twenty minutes to get the kids settled. Then I'll get our bags unpacked too. I may have a short rest before heading there."

"Sounds good," Nathan yelled at his two sons to stop while he caught up with them, then turned to Brianna and winked.

BRIANNA LEANED back in the driver's seat and closed her eyes, savoring the quiet. During the drive, her warnings to use inside voices had quickly been ignored. Tyler and Troy's incessant chatter had ceased to be charming hours ago, triggering a headache. After a pit stop in a rest area outside Sayward, the boys ran off their excess energy and then seemed ready to quieten down once back on the road. Thank God for technology. With the drop-down screen, she downloaded The Incredibles and Spirited Away movies. If that didn't keep their attention, at least it would lull them asleep. That strategy had worked, and now it would be Nathan's turn to keep them occupied. They had a great tag-team approach to their energetic boys.

When the crew finished the four o'clock loading, the BC Ferry left Port Hardy on the calm waters of the Inside Passage. Brianna finished putting the toiletries away and set fresh clothes out for the morning at the bottom of each bunk. Then she laid down, quickly lulled to sleep by the ferry's gentle rocking.

It seemed only a short time later that the door burst open with Tyler and Troy jumping on the bed beside her.

"Wake up! You're missing the best part. Come upstairs, Mom. Hurry, you're going to miss them."

Brianna opened her eyes and yawned, then smiled at her enthusiastic sons. "Miss what?" She gathered her boys into her arms and hugged them, even as they tried to wriggle out of her embrace.

"There's a tugboat out there, pulling hundreds and hundreds of logs. And two sea lions are sitting on them. They don't look like lions, but Dad says they are."

"Sounds like they're lazy, hitching a ride on a log boom." Brianna stretched. "Go on up, and I'll be there soon."

Brianna grabbed her camera to take shots of the event for her boys to remember. Searching the viewing area, it was easy to find her Irish lads. Troy sat atop his dad's shoulders, bouncing with excitement. His high pitch voice expressed the wonder of innocence, which made Brianna smile. Moving for a better angle, she snapped shots of her family on their maiden voyage. She caught Nathan's eyes and smiled.

"Worth it?" he mouthed, as their sons' chatter made conversation almost impossible.

"Definitely." Brianna slipped in next to him and hugged him as she surveyed the nearby mountainous coastline.

An announcement came over the public address system advising passengers that the dining facilities were now open. Gathering their sons, they found the spot where a buffet was available. The choices were limited but a welcome one after the long day of traveling and the recent hyperactivity. It wasn't long after that the boys were ready to head to their rooms, excited about the bunk bed arrangements.

As the ferry entered the open water between Vancouver Island and Calvert Island, the ride became choppier with rolling swells that the boys thought hilarious but only made Brianna feel nauseous. A short pillow fight and two trips to the washroom down the hall finally settled the boys into a deep sleep.

NATHAN KICKED the door open with his foot, bringing in three boxes in his arms. Looking for a place to stack them, he raised his eyebrows wordlessly, asking for direction.

"Living room. Where are the boys?" Brianna asked. She was not used to having them scatter out of sight in a strange setting.

"Over near the barn. Thomas brought in the mama sheep to milk. Lisa is showing the boys how to pet the lambs gently so they don't get frightened. Then she'll help feed the smallest ones before corralling them for the night. She's a cute kid, very helpful."

"I hope they're not in the way. This country life is exciting stuff for them, and they can be rambunctious."

"Thomas told me not to worry. He seems to enjoy watching their antics. He'll send them home with Lisa around five."

"Good. Thank God we brought two pairs of boots each for them. They're going to need them with all the animals around. I have to admit, it's been nice having people nearby to help with the kids, especially when it's so new to them. I'm not so worried that they'll get distracted and take off somewhere."

"Kari's also keeping an eye on them. She told me to let her know if there's anything else you need help with, she will come over."

"It was so considerate of her to have stocked the fridge with basics for us. And the ham she baked for us last night was delicious. We'll also have enough for dinner tonight."

"I'm sure we're going to notice a difference with the taste of fresh country supplies compared to supermarket food. Did you want to go to town tomorrow to fill our pantry and look around?"

"Maybe. We'll see how far we get with this unpacking. I brought the boxes of your research to the loft. And I found the one with linens. Can you make the bunk beds for the boys? One night on the floor with sleeping bags was fun, but I don't want a repeat performance tonight."

"On it. Did you find the bathroom supplies? We're all going to need showers tonight."

"I put the boxes marked bath in the tub, not sure if everything we need is in them, but it should be enough for tonight anyway." Brianna leaned against the kitchen counter and looked at her new living space. She blew a strand of hair out of her eyes, then looked over at her husband.

Nathan smiled. "So. Any regrets yet?" He went to the fridge, took out a Kokanee beer bottle, and tilted it towards her.

"Sure, I'd love one. I haven't stopped even once this afternoon." She screwed off the cap and clinked her bottle to his. "No regrets. Our future feels like an adventure. And so far, so good. I'm glad that we haven't had people popping in offering help. I know it's a friendly gesture, but right now, I need my space to figure things out."

"I hear you. I feel welcomed but not overwhelmed. That's a good start. When I finish setting up the beds, how would you like it if I started our first fire in our home? Apparently, the wood on the back porch was a freebie. When that's gone, I have to chop my own."

"Wonderful. No more work after dinner tonight. There's no point in rushing this. The boys will be excited about having an indoor fire. Too bad we didn't think of marshmallows. That would've been a great treat for them."

"There's always tomorrow. Thanks, Brianna. This research project wouldn't have happened without your support." Nathan leaned over and tilted her chin up to kiss her lips. "I love you more than you know, sweetheart."

Brianna put her hands on either side of his face. "Ditto. The possibilities for us are endless here. For ourselves, our kids, *and* our careers. The boys are going to do things they never even imagined. It will be quite the life." She wrapped her arms around his neck and hugged him tight for a long minute before releasing him and slapping his butt.

"Now go learn to be a chambermaid."

A WEEK LATER, the Cameron family felt entirely at home. They'd toured the retreat using a map showing the locations and purposes of the buildings and land. Matt had labeled the boundaries with information of neighboring farms and how to reach the town center or nearby points of interest.

Thomas refreshed Nathan and Brianna about safety procedures for operating the ATVs, then took them on a trail ride. After giving them maneuvering tips and observing them for a half-hour, he let them continue on their own. A few hours later, Brianna returned feeling excited and proud of her ability to navigate. True, she was much slower than Nathan, but she knew her comfort level and speed would improve with practice. After parking the vehicles near the hose next to the utility shed, she removed her helmet and gloves, glowing with excitement.

"Not bad for my first time," Brianna teased her husband. "It won't be long, and you'll be following my dust on the trails."

"Not likely. Seniority means I go first." Nathan looked around the shed and the compound. "It's sure beautiful here. I see they have four machines that can be signed out and reserved a week ahead, but I'm wondering if we should use a portion of our grant money to buy a couple of second-hand units for ourselves. If we don't, it might limit how spontaneous we can be to take the boys out. Or when we start researching. There are places we'll need to overnight to save travel hours. I wouldn't want to put anyone else out because we're using them regularly."

"That's a great idea. Ask Matt about it, see what he thinks. And Thomas may know where to get a deal. It could be a smart long-term investment for our research. The only expensive item you've bought so far was the Kohler binocular scope, so go ahead and do it."

"I probably will. I'll talk to the guys, get some feedback. I'll hose off the machines and put them away. I hope Tyler and Troy have behaved for Lisa. Make sure to mark her hours on our calendar. I don't want to take advantage of anyone here."

"I know. We'll figure it out. Plus, Matt has ideas for equitable ways for everyone to contribute their share, besides the token rent. It shouldn't be hard." Brianna heard her stomach growl and checked her watch. "Time for lunch— I'm starving. I'll get the boys and whip something up to eat while you hose down the machines. Deal?"

At his agreement, Brianna walked towards the barn first. The lambs were outside frolicking in the new grass, curious about everything around them while still running to their mothers' sides at any perceived threat. Soon, giggles erupted from inside, and Brianna knew where she'd find the boys. The chicks were now old enough to be picked up gently. Their down was so soft that one could spend hours petting and observing them. Tyler and Troy kept track of the new feathers that some were growing, even naming a couple of the chicks. The shy one that kept running away from them was Bashful. The biggest and, therefore, the bully who pecked at his competitors was identified as Doc.

Thomas leaned over the wooden three-foot wall, watching the boys interact while laughing along with them. When he noticed Brianna enter, he told them to say goodbye to their chicks and go to their mom.

"Kari picked up Lisa to go to town, so I offered to watch them. I've had so much fun watching these two mischievous imps explore the farm. It reminds me of what *joy* feels like. They're full of it. I'm starting to think I'd like a few children just like them. I might have to talk to Sonja about that soon."

"I've never seen them so excited. The boys can't wait to

get out of the house in the morning and go '*splore*. This community has been a real adventure for them, that's for sure. I'm glad we came. Do you think Sonja's ready for kids?"

"I hope so. We've talked about it. Sonja's almost thirty-one, and I'm in my early forties, so we can't wait much longer, or I won't be able to keep up. She's put me off a few times about getting married. Not sure what the issue is, but I haven't pushed her."

"Good. When Sonja's ready, she'll tell you. I wasn't ready to settle down when Nathan asked me either. We were engaged for several years before we tied the knot."

"Point taken. It is what it is." Thomas switched the subject by opening the wooden gate for her boys. "Let's go. Your mom's waiting. It's lunchtime." Thomas grasped an arm on each of them to hustle them out quickly before the chicks escaped. "Don't forget soap and water before you leave the barn."

"Hey, Mom." The high-pitched voices of her young sons made her smile broadly. Brianna crouched and braced herself for the charge as they ran to hug her. After she kissed them, she stood and slipped an arm around each of them to propel them to the deep sink where the boys found the soap and paper towels. Already, the strict rules for entering or exiting the barn were now routine for them. Hygiene was everything to keep both humans and animals healthy.

"How was your trip? Did you wipe out?" Tyler eyed his mom, looking for signs of a tumble.

"It was fun, and no, I didn't have an accident. Probably because I was a slowpoke, I'll get better the more I practice. When we master it, we'll take you boys for a trail ride."

"When? Tomorrow?" Troy jumped up and down, excited by the possibility.

"No. In a week or so. So many safety rules we need to

learn first. Now, are you hungry? Do you want to see if there are any eggs in the baskets at the henhouse? Or would you rather have grilled cheese?"

"Eggs!" Eagerly the boys ran towards the chicken coop and raised the lids on the outside baskets to check. They collected a cache of six eggs, and Brianna carried them in a pocket she made from the T-shirt she wore. She'd make an omelet for them, followed by toast and jam if they were still hungry. Some days they could pack the food away.

A WEEK LATER, Brianna nestled Troy in her arms while Nathan had Tyler asleep on his lap. The crackle and sizzle in the fireplace warmed the living room and created a peaceful end to their evening.

"Thank God we found Troy quickly." Brianna kept her voice low so the boys wouldn't wake up. "I'm still having a hard time understanding why he wandered away. He never leaves his brother's side."

"Oh, I think there's more to this story than they were telling us," Nathan whispered back. "Did you see the nervous looks they were giving each other? Something occurred between them, I'm sure of it. But I'll bet my last dollar it won't happen again. Tyler was truly in a panic when we couldn't find Troy, and he's been sticking like glue to his side ever since."

"Our boys have always been so close. I don't get it. What do you think? An adventure gone bad? A fight?"

"Either one." Nathan shifted the dead weight of his exhausted son to relieve the tingling in his thigh. "Troy was so tired that when it started to rain, he found a dry spot underneath an overturned tree stump and promptly fell asleep. And that boy can sleep through a thunderstorm and not wake up. Good thing the flashlight caught the reflector tape on his jacket."

"True, he wouldn't have heard us, and we'd still be looking. Thank God for our neighbors. Everyone came out with flashlights and helped with the search. He was only a half-mile from home, but it felt like a hundred." Brianna shivered as she recalled the terror she felt when Tyler returned from the main lodge alone.

"I'll bet they'll be telling us the whole story within a week. Right now, our sons are scared they'd be in trouble." Nathan awkwardly lifted Tyler into his arms and headed to the bedroom. "I'll come back and get Troy in a minute."

Brianna threaded her fingers through Troy's curly hair, still damp from the hot bath. His cheeks were flushed, and he was clutching his favorite stuffy close to him. Living in the country had seemed a harmless adventure until today, but now she had reservations. They'd have to enforce a strict buddy program between them. Accidents happen, and she didn't want to lessen her guard just because she felt the safety of her community protected them.

"I know I said I'd go with you to Nusatsum Falls tomorrow, but I can't," Brianna whispered as Nathan bent to retrieve Troy from her arms. "I want to stick close to home this week."

"That's fine. I'll stay home too."

Brianna watched her husband tuck the boys in bed and made sure he nestled the spotted Dalmatian in Troy's arms. They kissed their sons' goodnight, then returned to the living room.

"Want a beer or a glass of wine, sweetie?" Nathan was at the fridge looking for a snack to go with it.

"Sure, the wine's fine. And there are nuts in the

41

cupboard. About tomorrow—you can go on your own. You don't need to stay home with us. I have more than enough pictures of moss, mushrooms, and lichens from the last trip. I'd like to spend the day with the boys."

"I'll see how I feel about it in the morning. I have some slides I need to analyze and photograph. Don't worry, it wouldn't be a wasted day if I stayed home."

Brianna tilted her glass to her husband. "We've done well so far, haven't we? Hard to believe it's almost the middle of August already. Thomas says we have another six weeks to explore before the snow accumulates in the foothills."

"Our first winter should be interesting. Even though we had a scare today, I'm still confident about our decision to come here. We have so much work to coordinate our GPS readings with our samples that the winter will fly by. I'm so glad we bought our own ATVs. It's been great to have the freedom whenever we want. I have so many ideas and plans I want to outline for the spring to send to the research board for consideration."

"It's challenging with all the new opportunities. I know this has been a good move for the family. The boys will grow up with so many more experiences than they would have had if we'd stayed in Olympia." Brianna ran her hand over her hair, pleased with her decision to let her usually short hair grow longer for the cold winters they'd have here. She'd fight the curls with the longer length, but it wasn't so important anymore to have a sophisticated look she needed back home to be taken seriously. Her petite frame and youthful appearance that sometimes had undermined people's confidence wouldn't be a problem here.

Brianna had been surprised at the amount of involvement her husband now took around the house. Living here seemed to equalize the workload, whether it was professional or at home. Nathan would often catch her by surprise by prepping a meal while she was out helping with the communal garden or learning how to preserve the home-grown vegetables and fruit. Tyler and Troy were great helpers and enjoyed working alongside the older children like Lisa and Chloe.

Here was living proof of how villages could influence and raise children to be environmentally conscious and community-minded.

"Guess you're looking forward to Bruce and Erin arriving next month." Brianna snuggled with Nathan on the sofa, watching the fire die down. Red embers glowed as the firewood crumbled through the grate, its flaming energy spent. "Have they decided if they're staying with us or renting the tourist cabin?"

"They're taking the cabin for a week. Families get a reduced rate if the rental isn't already booked. Erin doesn't take time off very often, so they're blending the trip so they can see what we've got ourselves into. I'm sure you'll see her a lot, but she'll have her privacy when she wants it. Thomas was lucky and drew a moose, so Bruce is pretty excited. He's never hunted moose before."

"You're going with the guys too, aren't you?"

"Of course—although I don't plan on hunting. I'm along for the ride. It ought to be beautiful scenery. I'll man the overnight camp and keep the campfire going while they're out. I'll be the camp cook, poor guys. I'll bring slides and my camera, in case I get a chance to explore."

"You'll do fine. I'll give you a ziplock of spices for you to throw a stew or chili together, then they can eat anytime they get back. And if I'm not mistaken, you'll be eating game the following night."

"That's the plan. We'll be back by dinnertime on

Monday. Bruce wants to try river fishing after that. The steelhead salmon are fighters and much larger than Bruce is used to catching in Washington. That I'll do. I sure hope I can beat him at something this time."

"Why not ask Thomas? He'll probably give you good advice that will help. It might give you an advantage."

"Maybe. Bruce has always been crazy about fishing and hunting. He lives for it. Did I tell you he has two freezers at home? One for fish, the other for partridge and game. He swears he'll live to be a hundred on wild meat."

Brianna knew that Nathan often wondered at the difference between him and his brother, who was only four years older, but a whole generation wiser in everyday life. She smiled as she watched her husband stretch and yawn as the day's events caught up with him.

"Could be. I've read that cholesterol levels are much lower in deer and moose than beef. And everybody knows omega-3 oils in fish keep the heart-healthy. Not sure I'd want to live to be that age, but each to their own."

Brianna watched her husband stoke the embers and shut the glass doors on the fireplace. She loved relaxing around a cozy fire, something she'd never experienced before. "Do you think your brother and his wife would consider moving here? There are still two or three empty homes. I think you and the boys would enjoy having family here. It wouldn't be so lonely. And you never know, he might enjoy going on some of your longer explorations."

"I'm keeping my fingers crossed. The lifestyle appeals to Bruce, and he'd be a great help for me. I'm not so sure about Erin."

"Why not? She's been successful with her cookbooks on Amazon, and she can work on that from anywhere. Erin could probably even expand and add books on cooking wild game. That might give her a niche market. With her background culinary skills, it wouldn't take her long to get a collection together. With the right marketing on Facebook and her website, she could be tempting a new audience six months before she publishes."

"It wouldn't surprise me if she's already considered that. I know that they've had run-ins near their home in Yakima with climate refugees. They're not too happy with the way things are going. He sent me videos of protests at city hall. A lot of angry people there too."

"Isn't that weird—that phrase is heard so much nowadays, yet it's something that we never used to hear about—at least not in our country. These are scary times. I hope by the time we're ready to head back, the government has figured out a solution to this. It's beautiful here, but I'm a proud American. I want to go back home, eventually. Anna agrees with me on this, although she's asked me not to broadcast it. Matt's still convinced worse times are coming."

"Nothing we can do about it. Climate change is here, and we have to adapt. It just came much quicker than we thought it would. Like Matt told me, we've all stuck our heads in the sand for way too long. Now nature's paying us back and forcing us to change our habits."

"Call me an optimist, but every time there's been a huge problem, we've pulled together and made our way through it. Depressions, wars, hurricanes...we're down for a while, but we get up, figure it out, and get back on our feet. We will again."

Nathan drained the last of his beer, took the empty wineglass she'd been fiddling with, and put them on the coffee table. "Now that we've solved America's problems let's go to bed. I have another problem that needs fixing."

Nathan smiled with his lopsided grin and tilted his head, questioning her response.

"I can fix anything you can throw at me, Mr. Cameron. Lead me on." Brianna giggled as Nathan dragged her off the sofa and down the hall.

CHAPTER 3 - THE ZANETTIS

Pete Zanetti rolled down the door to the U-Haul truck and secured it with a lock. He waved goodbye to his wife, Denyse, and their daughter, Chloe. One waved, the other turned her face. Whatever. Pete was tired of pussy-footing around his fifteen-year-old daughter. If she thought she was going to win this, she was sadly mistaken. This new future was *his* time. He opened the driver's door and hoisted himself up into the driver's seat.

"Ready?" Pete looked over to his twelve-year-old son, Mike.

Thank God he was excited about the move. His left knee bouncing up and down was proof of it.

"I was ready yesterday. This has been the longest day of my life." Mike's blue eyes sparkled with anticipation. Ever since they began talking about going to Bella Coola, his son —the google expert—had turned into an encyclopedia. He studied British Columbia's coastline and the route the ferry would use to bring them there. He explored sites of interest in Tweedsmuir Provincial Park, where he hoped they would spend a lot of time. And he researched the Nuxalk First Nations history.

"We're going to see some beautiful country on the way there. It's going to be hectic for the next three or four days, and I hope you're ready for that."

"No problem, Dad. Just tell me what you want me to do. I'm strong, and I want to help as much as I can."

Pete smiled at his son, going through the gawky stage, all long legs, and big feet. "I know, son. I appreciate your work so far. You've been a big help. And don't worry, when we get settled, we'll be checking out everything around us. I think you're going to love it. I'm hoping it'll inspire me to start writing again." Turning on the radio station, he effectively switched the subject.

WHEN PETE DECIDED to find out about his birth parents through Ancestry DNA, the result had surprised him. Although afterward, he realized he shouldn't have been. His dark brown, almost obsidian eyes and hair, coupled with his high cheekbones, gave hints of his heritage.

As a very young toddler, the Zanetti's adopted him. They had one son named Marco but were unable to conceive more children. Wanting Marco to have a brother, they decided to adopt. They started a winery that would pass from generation to generation, just as his parents had done in the old country. Having another son to share the load made sense to them.

Pete had a happy childhood near Cultus Lake. Paol and Rosanna's parents were 'hobby' farmers whose mission was to develop a winery like his paternal grandfather's in Italy. Young and adventurous, Paol and his wife had immigrated from Liguria, near Genoa, after the war. When he came to British Columbia's Lower Mainland, he searched for property near the mountains that could be terraced, just as his parents' vineyard had been. Although it didn't border the sea, he bought the land surrounding Teapot Hill near Cultus Lake. The lake brought the necessary breeze in the hot summers to provide the perfect environment for Vermentino grapes.

In the early years, Paol and Rosanna grew blueberries on their flat acreage for market to generate the funds for their fledgling winery. He also blasted a cave near the bottom of their hill to hold the oak barrels he hoped to need one day.

Then Paol began the laborious job of clearing and terracing the slope. He journeyed back to Liguria for several years to see his parents, returning with vine cuttings from his father's farm. Using hardworking laborers from the Sikh community, they coaxed the vines to maturity. Eventually, he taught his son, Tony, to air dry the grapes in layers for three to six months until the sugars concentrated to 15%. Pressing the grapes gently, he monitored for sweetness and alcohol, then contained the wine in oak barrels to age. Pete's parents continued to cultivate the vines, and thirty years later, the vines were well established and producing beautiful wines.

Paol and Rosanna retired in 1990, leaving the winery to their oldest son, Marco. They had wanted Pete to partner with his brother in the winery, but Pete wasn't interested. He wanted more out of life than worrying about the weather, yield, or the bottling and marketing. Pete gladly gave it up to Marc. He could have it all.

In fairness, Pete's parents had left him a ten-acre parcel of land near Mission. Pete leased it out to neighbors for growing corn and found his niche at UBC, where he studied literature. A few years later, he met Denyse at an Anglican church ceremony when his father died. She was studying to become a theologian. Their discussions of male/female roles prompted many heated exchanges and acted like an irresistible magnet, which resulted in their marriage almost twenty years ago.

They made a good life for themselves in Kerrisdale, a short distance from UBC, where he eventually earned a position as a professor of modern literature. And of course, many things Pete had hoped to accomplish were postponed when Chloe was born, followed two years later with Mike.

Now it was his time to put himself first. Strange how it sometimes took traumatic news to make one re-assess their personal situation and needs. He had attributed his constant fatigue with his new position as Associate Director of the Arts program. Then one morning, Pete noticed a swollen gland on his neck behind his right ear. His diagnosis of acute myeloid leukemia six months ago was shocking. After a bone marrow test that identified cancer, it took him an entire month to come to grips with it and tell Denyse.

Denyse and Dr. Weldon encouraged him as he began a series of chemotherapy treatments. After follow-up testing, Pete took a leave of absence from the university to concentrate on the recommended radiation therapy to stop the acceleration of rising white blood cell counts. Occasionally, Pete would have a deep ache in his bones, but his chief complaint was fatigue. And yet, some days, he felt so well that he wondered if they hadn't misdiagnosed him.

Bless her heart, Denyse agreed that it wasn't time to tell the kids yet. That would only accomplish needless worry. The disease could last a year, or it could last five years. New treatments were evolving all the time. It all depended on the progression. In the meantime, he didn't want his children looking at him with pity, nor did he want to waste any more time.

How lucky were they that Pete was recruited for a soccer scholarship at the University of Washington? Who would have foreseen the tie he and Matt Taylor developed while sharing a dorm? Over the years, they kept up with each other at alumni functions, occasionally holidaying together.

With Facebook, they stayed in touch. When Pete saw the move Matt's family had made, he contacted his old friend via Messenger. After several Zoom conversations and prayerful conversations with Denyse and Matt, Pete decided to join the group. He applied for an extended absence to pursue his lifelong goal of writing the great Canadian novel in a calm and peaceful environment. Denyse was optimistic that combined with a diet that would be organic and healthier than what they'd grown accustomed to, it might make a positive difference to Pete's health.

Pete drove along the #1 freeway west to Horseshoe Bay, where they would board to cross the Salish Sea to Vancouver Island. They often came to the Island, at least every few years, to enjoy the wild west coast of Tofino-Ucluelet. This time they'd be heading to the very northern tip of the Island and boarding another ferry from Port Hardy to their new home.

"Aren't you excited to get there, Dad? You don't look very cheerful."

"Sorry, that's not it at all. I'm thrilled about this move. I'm just tired." Pete glanced over at his son and forced a smile to put his son at ease. "No worries, Mike. Once we get there and settled, I'll be more energetic. You'll see."

"Ok, Dad. I think everyone's happy except for Chloe. She can sure be grumpy."

"I know. But she's leaving friends behind who mean a lot to her, so she's nervous about that. I think once she's been there a while, she'll adjust."

"So, I know you've got time off to write a book. What's it going to be about?"

"Not sure yet. I've had a manuscript that I've been working on for years about families coming to B.C. I'm hoping I'll be able to salvage some of that and continue. It was going to be factual about the different cities sprouting up from the Gold Rush until after the population boom of the 50s. But something has been telling me to make it more personal." Pete turned to his gifted son and winked. "And what are you looking forward to doing once we're settled?"

"I want to learn to drive ATVs and ride horses. We're so close to Tweedsmuir Park, and I'm hoping we can go exploring and see stuff. Ever since I found out I'm part of First Nations, I'd like to see what their life is like too. Maybe you'll even write about your heritage."

"Who knows? It sounds like a long list of wants you've got there. Close to three-quarters of the population in Bella Coola are Nuxalk, so you'll probably have some as friends. Just don't go asking too many questions. Let them share things as they get to know you. Otherwise, they might feel that they're just a research project. That wouldn't go over well."

"Of course! I get that, and I'm not *that* dumb." Mike turned to his iPhone and plugged it into the dashboard to recharge. Searching for his playlist, he soon popped in his earbuds and zoned out.

Denyse texted Kari to meet them at the tourist bureau when they arrived in Bella Coola. When she pulled her red Toyota SUV in behind Pete's U-Haul, Kari and Lisa waited outside their car and waved to them. Pete and Mike waved from inside the U-Haul but refrained from getting out.

"Welcome, Denyse—you made it. I'll bet you never thought you'd get here, right?" Kari held her arms out to Denyse and pulled her in for a hug. "That's the way I felt at first. I wondered what kind of crazy idea Matt and Ray had pushed us into. Now, I'm more than good with it."

"I agree, it was a dramatic decision to uproot our life in Kerrisdale to come here, but I'm looking forward to it. It's what our family needed. We've never seen such beautiful scenery. The trip was simply majestic." Denyse looked back over her shoulder and beckoned Chloe to come outside their SUV. Chloe shook her head and looked away from them.

"I'm sorry, Lisa. I'm sure she remembers you from the week we spent together on the alumni retreat near Tofino a few years ago. I've never seen her so rude and upset since she realized we were seriously packing and moving here."

"Not to worry. It took a while for me too. It was hard leaving my friends and my mom. I miss them a lot. I'm sure glad to see another girl come to live in our community. We'll get together another day." Lisa shrugged off Chloe's manners and returned to their vehicle.

"I'll be happy to see my sister arrive too. It'll make an enormous difference to have Anna here with Lisa. Teen years are so dramatic for girls, and I'm not used to dealing with that."

"No kidding." Denyse lowered her voice and motioned Kari to the side. "You know Pete isn't well, don't you?"

"Yes, Matt told me. Only the four of us are aware of it. No

one else is aware. It's up to you whether you want anyone else to know."

"Good, because my kids don't even know how sick their dad is. This trip has been exhausting for him, and I'm worried."

"Matt figured it might be tough, so he's asked Thomas and Nathan to help unload your truck. Then you can take your time organizing things while Pete catches his breath. If you need any other help, just let me know. We don't want to overwhelm our new members by being on their porch every day."

"Thanks, Kari. That's very thoughtful of you."

"No problem. There are basics in the fridge and a large roasting chicken in the oven. I prepped vegetables for you to throw in for the last hour or so of cooking. I hope you enjoy it. If you're ready, follow me. It's about fifteen minutes from here."

Tears came to Denyse's eyes. "That's awesome. Thanks again." She gave Kari another hug, then returned to her car.

The trio of vehicles made their way slowly through Bella Coola, viewing their new town. The only one who wasn't eyeing up both sides of the road was Chloe. She was busy trying to text her friends and growling when the signal was lost.

"We're in the flipping boonies, Mom. I can't live in a place that doesn't have coverage. How am I going to keep in touch with my friends?"

"It won't be easy, but there's a cell tower in Hagensborg. You'll figure it out. We warned you it wouldn't be as convenient as home, but you will still be able to FaceTime with your friends in the evenings now and then. Don't worry about it. Look around you, Chloe. This area is your new home, and it's beautiful."

"Really? Not *my* idea of beautiful, Mom. Why did we have to come here anyway? Dad could've written a book at home for crying out loud. I don't get it." Chloe stomped her foot on the floor mat and glared at her mom.

"Give it a chance, Chloe. Please? You might surprise yourself."

WHAT A DIFFERENCE A MONTH MAKES. Pete sighed a breath of relief. The sun was warm on his face as he gazed skyward towards Kalone Peak. The faint sound of a power saw that Ray and Nathan were using was discernable as they fell timber to dry for winter firewood. Pete was thankful for their generous offer to take Mike after he begged to accompany them. Armed with safety gear and assurances that he would follow directions, Mike hopped on the back of an ATV and waved goodbye to his parents with a huge grin on his face. Another good sign.

Seeing his daughter not only excited about exploring possibilities but volunteering for chores had also eased his worries. The move definitely hadn't started well, but Jed and Aaron, who were over a year older than Chloe, had gone out of their way to make her and her brother feel welcome. Watching her growing enthusiasm warmed Pete's heart. Of course, being summer made the options more manageable. It might be a different story once the cold, short winter days arrive. Chloe might be craving the city life of Kerrisdale by then and driving them crazy. However, Pete was concentrating on the here and now, hoping the future would look after itself.

For now, Chloe sported a smile and enthusiasm for her new home. She took on sharing duties of feeding the lambs and chickens. On weekends, Lisa had given her riding lessons on a gentle mare named Daisy. Holding Daisy's bridle, Lisa made sure that Chloe was comfortable riding in the saddle. She taught her the basics of using her knees to guide the horse and the best way to use the reins gently to steer Daisy in a specific direction. When Chloe felt comfortable, Lisa rode her mom's horse alongside her through the meadows and eventually into the foothills. Now at the dinner table, the sullen teenager had disappeared, replaced with an excited Chloe who regaled her family with her new skills. Her iPhone was often left at home, no longer her security blanket.

Pete leaned against his hoe, watching his daughter join the teenagers for her first full day of adventure on the ATVs. She sat behind Jed, hanging on for dear life, while Lisa sat behind her cousin Aaron. After reassurances from the boys that they wouldn't scare her with antics, Chloe had finally agreed to the trip to a local watering hole on the Nusatsum River. With their backpacks filled with drinks, lunch, and swim gear, Chloe vibrated with nervous excitement. Wonders of wonders, he and Denyse would have the whole day free to themselves. He waved goodbye to the group, then checked the time.

Pete removed his gloves and examined the blisters that were healing. It wouldn't be long before they'd be calloused, just like his father's hands from working on his vineyard. If anyone would've told him he'd be a farmer one day, he would've bet his life savings they were wrong. And yet, here he was. Putting his gear away, he went back home ready to spend time on his computer, outlining characters for his new book plot.

Surveying the land around him, Pete acknowledged he was beginning to accept his limitations, making the best of an uncontrollable situation. This morning he had cultivated six rows of carrots, beets, and bush beans. At the end of each row, he took a short break. Denyse always made him smoothies made of fruit, Greek yogurt, and protein powder that she believed would strengthen him. He was supposed to snack on the ziplock of dried fruit and nuts in his pocket, yet sometimes it was a struggle with a dwindling appetite. But he didn't believe in giving up and did his best to maintain his health.

Every third day was their schedule for garden maintenance, which had worked out well so far. After lunch, Denyse would continue while Pete had a shower and catnapped for an hour before working on his book outline. The frantic pace of his previous life had disappeared, and he was surprised that he didn't miss it. Then if he had the energy, he would prep dinner for Denyse to finish later.

Pete felt strong arms encircle his waist and his wife's breasts against his back. He warmed to her touch and thanked God for her no-nonsense approach to his health. He was sure that she noticed the weight he had lost and just as confident that she'd convinced herself it was due to the physical labor he was now engaged in. Pete turned to hold her in his arms and tilted his head to one side. "Are you coming to relieve me?"

"Soon. I saw the kids leaving. It seems like they've adjusted quite quickly. It looks like Chloe's happy now. I wonder if she'll be just as happy when we ask her to help in the vegetable garden. I worry how she's going to handle seeing her chicks and lambs grow to become our dinner." Denyse lifted her eyebrows for Pete's opinion,

"I'm sure she'll be upset at first, just like anybody else. She'll probably follow the lead of the other kids and eventually realize it's part of life. As far as gardening, Matt's scheduling the kids for an hour a couple of times a week, which will be an easy introduction. Once she sees the other kids pitching in, she won't think twice about it."

"You're looking good today, Pete. You're tanning nicely, albeit a farmer's tan. There's a definite difference where the brim of your hat protects your forehead and where your short sleeves protect your arms. Cute."

"Cute? Don't make me laugh. Can you imagine my colleagues seeing me like this? I would be the topic of conversation for sure."

"Who cares? It's good for you. You're already stronger than you first were when we started gardening. By the way, don't forget I'm taking you to town for your blood tests in the morning. They'll forward the results to your specialist, who will probably be surprised about your improvement."

"I hope so. Of course, sitting on my ass in the university didn't earn me any muscles, so I'm bound to get stronger working physically. As long as I get a short rest in the afternoon, I feel good. Keep your fingers crossed." Pete crossed his own and kissed them, making his wife smile.

"I'm happy that you've started forming a plotline and characters for your book. You're balancing this life quite nicely. Every day, I thank the Lord for Matt and Anna. This lifestyle is just what you need. When things slow down late in September, you'll be all set to jump into your novel. I like seeing you sit on the porch with your laptop."

"I've kind of surprised myself. I never expected to fit into this place so quickly. Maybe I'm absorbing the ambiance of our new lifestyle. I wondered whether I'd be bored here, but that hasn't been an issue so far. And when the muse comes on strong in the fall, you'll have to twist my arm to do anything else. She's quite the taskmaster." Pete returned the hug and whispered in her ear. "Thank you."

"For what? You haven't tasted my chili yet. It might be too spicy for you."

"Not that, silly. Thank you for supporting my wish to come here. At first, the decision was all about me and following my dream and handling this sickness. But now, I can see it was a great decision, not only for me but for all of us."

Denyse hooked her hand into the crook of his arm and headed towards home and lunch. "You're welcome. I believe God answered our prayers when we asked Him what to do. He guided us, and, as usual, His direction was for the greater good. Didn't I tell you to trust Him? Who do you think planted your idea?"

"I guess so. I'm leaning your way more and more. I'm just glad I had kept up with Matt from our early days at the University. Otherwise, this probably wouldn't have happened."

Pete enjoyed a small bowl of his wife's chili with a tall glass of milk. He watched her put the bowls and utensils in a soapy sink of hot water afterward, then after kissing his cheek, she headed back to the field. Pete washed the dishes, and set them to dry, then retreated to the shower. Later, he collapsed in his bathrobe on the bed for a much-needed nap, at peace with his world.

MIKE WORE earmuffs to deaden the shrill whine of the power saw Nathan was using to de-limb the trees they had fallen. Once he moved from one alder to another, Mike would help haul the branches away to a burn pile fifty feet away. Surrounded by large river rocks dragged by the ATV, it was fifteen feet across. Ray had a two-horsepower water pump in the creek, with a fifty-foot canvas fireman's hose connected for fire safety. This site was one they'd used before, far enough from the woods and close to the creek.

After giving Mike safety instructions, the experienced woodsman had started a low fire, showing him how to feed the branches into the middle of the fire once the long limb had burned through the middle.

It was hot, sweaty work. A man's job. It was true that a man would probably do it much quicker than he could. Nevertheless, his contribution made him feel good. A tap on his shoulder startled him. Mike slid his earmuffs down onto his neck to hear what was going on.

"Lunch time. I put our backpacks in the shade by the ATVs, and we'll eat there. I'll turn the water pump on, then I want you to douse the perimeter of the firepit as I showed you, OK? Do you think you need help?" Ray cocked his head to one side, giving Mike the chance to handle the job himself.

"No, it's not hard. It won't take me long."

"Good. When you finish that, put your hardhat and gear aside and join us. Have you been drinking your water?"

"Yes. I'm on my third bottle already. Working in this heat sure makes you thirsty."

"It's the sweat from working too. You can lose a few pounds of water in a day doing work like this, so if you don't keep hydrating, you're at risk for passing out or having a heat stroke."

"That makes sense. I'll soak the area around the pit, then I'll be right there. I'm starving." Mike circled the burn pile and pushed the longer sticks into the fire with his steel pike pole while Ray started the pump up. When Mike felt the tap on his shoulder, Ray gave the thumbs-up sign and pointed to the hose, then headed to his ATV for lunch.

The water pressure had mounted, and when Mike turned on the nozzle, the force it produced surprised him. He walked along the perimeter, keeping his hose a foot from the ground and drenching the soil till it pooled. Mike chuckled to himself as his stomach growled. He'd never been as hungry as he was now, but he'd never worked this hard either.

After finishing the job, Mike went back to the creek and flicked the switch off. Thank goodness, his ears already had enough noise today. Mike walked towards Ray and Nathan and took his heavy work gloves off. He placed them with his hardhat and muffs on top of the last log that had been limbed. Following Nathan to the ATVs, Mike joined him to wash up, splashing water on his face and hands. Ray was already there, laying out their packs.

"You didn't discard your empty bottles, did you?" Ray asked.

"I put them where you guys put yours. I figured that'd be ok."

"It is. When we finish lunch, I'd like you to get all those bottles, and we'll fill them from the cooler jug we brought with us. You'll see we're big on reusing and recycling around here."

"Ok." Mike bit into his egg sandwich his mom made him, barely taking the time to chew it. Suddenly, he was ravenous. Good thing that his mom had packed him three sandwiches. He'd eat them all, then finish his lunch with homemade brownies she'd made last night.

"Mike...slow down, son. You'll get cramps when you go back to work if you eat too fast. The food won't disappear. We'll take a full half-hour rest before we start working again. Relax." Ray winked at him. "You've worked like a trooper this morning. Good job. You'll be sporting muscles soon with that kind of workout."

"Do you think I can come again? I'd rather do this than garden, that's for sure."

"It's ok by me, but you'll have to check with your parents. Nothing wrong with gardening. It's backbreaking work if you aren't careful. Although it feels good when you start harvesting and know you're part of the reason everyone is eating well."

"I guess so. Dad seems to like it. He never gardened at home. He didn't even mow the lawn. Chloe or I did it, so it seems strange to see him working in it. He's different here."

"Good different?" Nathan asked as he munched on an apple for his dessert.

"Yea. He talks to us more than he used to. He's lightened up. Dad's not so serious and stressed out like when he was at the University."

"Then it sounds like this was a good move for your family."

"Looks like it. Even Chloe is more cheerful, and I almost like her." Mike felt his eyebrows lift in surprise over how well he was getting along with his sister.

"Another month and you older kids will start going into town for school. How do you feel about that?"

"Fine. I'm glad the school board included grade eight in McKenzie High. At least I'll see the kids from here. If I were in grade seven, I'd be stuck at the Elementary school. I guess there aren't enough kids to have a larger range middle school in Bella Coola."

"That's true. Have you seen the curriculum for Sir Alexander Mackenzie School?"

"I googled it. Looks ok. Small classes, but that doesn't bother me. Ever since I found out that my dad has a First

Nations background, I've been interested in learning more about it. They have an elective called Nuxalk language and culture. I'm hoping I can register."

"Hmm. It would help if you talked to Thomas and Sonja then. They have several friends who are active Nuxalk members. They might give you information before school starts that will help you fit in quicker."

"Do they have a longhouse?" Mike's voice rose an octave with his excitement. He jumped to his feet and wandered about, unable to contain himself. "What about totem poles?"

"Hold everything, Mike. We'll tell Thomas that you're interested in learning more and let him approach his friends. Sonja teaches Science and takes her classes on hikes to observe geology and the environment. Maybe we can get them to organize a group hike with a Nuxalk guide to see the petroglyphs and other historical sites. I'm sure she'll appreciate your keen interest."

Nathan smiled at the enthusiasm Mike displayed. "I might just try and organize another hike and show our community what I do when I'm gathering my research on species at risk. What do you think?"

"Sounds great. I'll bet everyone at our place will come. Well, maybe not my dad, or Mr. and Mrs. Devries, but almost everyone."

"How does your dad feel about you getting involved with the Nuxalk Nation? Is he interested too?" Ray questioned as he stepped in to slow Mike's incessant chatter. The food and rest had re-energized his young helper.

"He doesn't say much. He loved his adoptive mom and dad, but I think it always bothered him that he was adopted. That's why he took the DNA test. He looked a lot like his Italian parents, so he thought he had a Mediterranean background. He was a little surprised, although once he knew for sure, he could see the resemblance. Dad knows I've been snooping around the different bands on the west coast since we found out. I've asked him if we should look into an ancestry site for a blood relative, but he doesn't want to. My dad says he has the answer now, and he's satisfied with the family he was raised with."

"Ok, well, before I talk to Thomas, I think I'll have a chat with him and make sure he approves of making contact with the Nuxalk." Ray stood up and packed the garbage into a bag on the ATVs.

"Ok. But I know Dad won't care, he likes it when I'm researching anything. My dad says that it's good for the mind to expand its horizons or something like that. Should I collect the water bottles and fill them?"

"Yup, it's time to start work."

Ray returned to the area they had been falling in to assess the next cut. Standing back, he looked at the alder tree's natural stance. Ray waited until Nathan and Mike donned their gear and moved out of the way. With the coast clear, he started his power saw and cut a horizontal line two feet up from the ground. Then he carved an angular cut ten inches above that and continued sawing until he reached the horizontal cut. The wedge popped out with little effort.

"Keep behind me. Here goes another one!" Ray tickled the opposite side of the wedge until the tree's weight collapsed from the missing support. The crash onto the forest floor was thunderous.

"Your turn." Ray shut off his saw and moved away, letting Nathan begin the task of chopping off the branches. They worked well as a team, falling, limbing, then stacking the logs to dry. Soon Ray was searching for the next decent size alder to remove, and once again, a subsequent crash disturbed the tranquility of the hillside.

"One more Nathan, then I'll circle back and help limb. We'll call it quits after that. Okay with you?"

"Sure. A cold beer is going to taste good when we get home."

"Definitely. Are you up for a swim before we get back?"

"I am!" Mike's energy had waned. He was dragging the branches away at a slower pace than he had this morning, which wasn't surprising. He was determined not to give up, so he pushed himself to continue. As he looked towards the area they had cut that morning, he scrunched his eyes, trying to make out what he was seeing.

"Ray! Ray! I think I see smoke over by those logs. Ah shit! I swear I soaked the pit really good."

"Nathan, run and move the pump upstream closer to that smoke, then start it up. Mike, come with me."

"Honest, Ray, I soaked it all the way around those rocks." Mike's voice quivered as his eyes flitted between the smoke and Ray's face.

"I believe you, Mike. It was probably a spark that became airborne and landed in our debris pile. I should've known better than to start even a small burn today. Thank God you caught sight of it."

Ray ran to the ATVs and put on his safety gear, gathering two shovels before running towards the swirling smoke. "Get your gear on and get to the creek. Start hauling the hose as Nathan moves the pump. Stay close to either Nathan or me. I want you in my sight line at all times. Concentrate on spraying water anywhere that looks suspicious."

Mike geared up and started dragging the canvas water hose. He glanced over to the creek, where he saw Nathan splashing through the creek bed, obviously moving the pump and dragging the connected hose along with it. He ran to the burn pile and wrapped as much hose as he could handle around his shoulders, and pulled it upstream.

Nathan dropped the pump parallel to the recently felled trees and hurried over to help Mike. "Heavier than it looks, isn't it?"

"I'll say. Nathan, I soaked—"

"I know, Mike. Even though it's cold at night, the daytime heat dries these woods up pretty quick. It's our fault. We shouldn't have even had the small fire we did." Nathan was puffing as he talked, the exertion of running with heavy items making him lose his breath. "Thank God, there's no wind. We might get lucky."

Watching Ray smack the smoking debris, then lifting branches and clearing them from the area, gave Mike the clue he needed to help. As Nathan ran back to start the pump, Mike imitated Ray, brushing aside debris with his shovel. The now welcome noise of the pump caused Ray to turn and nod. "Pull the hose as close as you can get, and turn it on full blast once you see the pressure has built up. Nathan will help me with smothering and spreading the piles."

Mike dropped the shovel and ran back to get the hose, only coming as close as thirty feet from the area. He heard Nathan shouting as he came near and turned to see him pointing to another swirl of smoke rising right behind Ray.

Feeling the pressure build, Mike opened the nozzle and concentrated on the closest plume, dousing it quickly. Ray turned and saw the drenched area and nodded to Mike, then pointed further ahead. Mike redirected the water to the next swirl of smoke, attempting to avoid Ray and Nathan, but it was impossible. They concentrated their efforts near the limbs that they hadn't yet moved, and their bodies were soon wet as well.

Half an hour later, a smoky, steamy Ray came and spoke with Mike. "Good job, son. Can you manage this for a while more? Nathan and I will get the ATVs, and we'll move the debris field near the creek. We'll keep the water on it for an hour and check for hot spots. We were lucky. I don't know what we were thinking, falling at this time of year. Wait till Thomas comes home from fishing the coast. He's going to have our asses."

A FEW HOURS LATER, the adrenaline rush had passed, and all three guys looked grimy and exhausted. The guys graded a full acre of ground with the help of ropes and ATVs, spreading the debris on the rocks near the creek. The land itself resembled a giant puddle. Overkill, to be sure, but one that suited them. Better safe than sorry.

Ray looked over to see Mike leaned against the ATV he had just loaded and wiped his forehead. Ray gathered up the rest of their gear and called Nathan to hop in. They headed to the creek and retrieved the pump, then wound up the fireman's hose, strapping it to the back of the ATV.

"The kid's beat. He did great today. I hope his dad isn't going to kill us."

"I'm sure he's going to have some choice words, as will everyone else at home. How stupid were we?" Nathan's voice was gravelly, likely from dehydration and inhaled smoke.

"And I deserve every bit of shit I get. We'll come back tomorrow and check this over and keep an eye on it for a week or so. I'll make it up to them, though. I don't know how, but I will. And I hope Pete'll be happy with the way his son behaved today. He listened and worked bravely."

"Thirteen-year-olds don't seem to be the same as when we were thirteen. You wouldn't have caught me working like that when I was Mike's age."

"No doubt." Ray yelled to Mike as they got nearer, "Hey Mike, what do you say? Shall we head out to Snootli Creek? It's deeper and flows into the Bella Coola River. We'll freshen up there before going home. What do you think?"

Shouts of agreement from Nathan and Mike made Ray laugh. Considering the type of lifestyle Nathan was used to as a botanist, he'd adjusted well to the physical demands of contributing to the Safe Haven's work routine. And now, Nathan could add the experience of fighting a brush fire. He wouldn't forget this day anytime soon. Although Ray was sure, he'd be happy to get back to documenting and collecting specimens tomorrow.

SLIPPING out of her jean cutoffs, Chloe pulled her T-shirt over her head, exposing the two-piece bathing suit she'd bought last year. She should probably order a new one. Her body shape had changed a fair amount in that brief amount of time. She never used to have cleavage or have to worry about her butt cheeks showing. Now she was always pulling or tugging at her suit to cover herself better. But these boys had been like older brothers to her—until today.

Chloe felt her face flush as she wondered what Jed thought of her and if he was feeling the same way she was. She'd caught him looking at her when he thought she wasn't, and it made her pulse race. Although Lisa was almost two years younger than her, they got along famously.

Shouting and splashing with each other had been a hoot until she caught Jed's eyes. Chloe looked down and saw the cold water had hardened her nipples into nubs, so she pulled her arms to her chest as she wiped the water from her face. She ran out of the water and toweled herself dry before throwing the T-shirt overtop. How embarrassing.

"So, tell me about the high school in town. Like how many kids are there?" Chloe wanted to move the conversation towards something different.

Lisa shrugged. "Not many. About a hundred kids, from Hagensborg, Four-mile Reserve, and a handful of other villages in the valley. It isn't hard to get help from the teacher compared to back home. Anybody who needs extra help or wants to excel gets all the support they want. There's also a First Nations School called the *Learning Place* that goes from Kindergarten to grade twelve too, which teaches about another hundred kids."

"It must get boring then. It's such a small town, and it doesn't look like there's much to keep us interested." Chloe's lower lip was beginning to pout as she thought of all the things she would've done at home.

Jed had become protective of his new home. "It's not so bad. There's a four-day music festival coming up in a few weeks. Like they have this thing every July, and local bands from all over the Coastal region enter and perform. I've heard it's a lot of fun, lots of people come and camp or stay with relatives around here. Then there's a three-day rodeo in August, with people from all over BC coming to compete. It's quite the party."

"That might be fun. I've played the guitar for five or six years now. Maybe I'll find a group that wants another member." Chloe felt her heart beat faster at the thought of joining a band. "Might not be so horrible after all."

"Then you should look into the local arts programs that usually start in the fall. In July and August, there's a market on Wednesday nights with music and entertainment. It's a jam session, so it's a good place to meet kids. For a small town, there's a lot to choose from. It's not that bad, Chloe. In the summertime, families are busy hiking to the falls or ATVing or fishing. Thomas told me mountain biking is taking off in the last few years too."

"Yea, my dad's excited about trying that. There are so many trails to explore, just as good as around Whistler. Dad bought us all new bikes for coming up here, but my dad's bike is electric—do you believe it? Do you guys mountain bike?"

"Sometimes. How come your dad got an electric bike?"

"I don't know. Something about low iron in his blood. He gets tired easily."

"That's too bad. Aaron and I haven't done much mountain biking. Whenever we have a choice, we like to take out the ATVs." Jed smirked. "We have a need for speed."

Aaron laughed as he punched Jed lightly in the shoulder. "Go ahead, tell her who the best ATV operator is in the snow?"

"It might be different this year. I was nervous last year, that's all." Jed's face grew red at Aaron's teasing.

Chloe wondered what the competition was all about. Jed seemed embarrassed. He was so cute when he blushed. "So, that's all we do in winter? Trail riding like today is a lot of fun, but I'm not so sure it'd be something I'd want to do when it's freezing out." Chloe leaned back onto her towel and looked up at the mountains that seemed so close she could almost touch them.

The mountain ranges would be spectacular with snow on them, although she'd probably prefer to look at them from inside their cabin. "Dad's after me to try cross-country skiing. I might try that." Chloe shrugged her shoulders as she looked over at Jed. "Would you come with me?"

Aaron butted into the conversation. "Are you kidding? Of course! I'm signing up for an outdoor education program through the high school. Why don't we all register for it? We get all sorts of opportunities to try different things that way, and it doesn't cost a cent."

Lisa and Jed jumped in, eager to plan for the long winter.

Eventually, as their full tummies lulled Lisa and Aaron into a light slumber, and Jed eyed Chloe with a questioning glance.

"What?"

"Just wondering if you'd be interested in teaching me how to play the guitar? Why don't you bring it out to the next bonfire and play for us?"

"Maybe. I could try anyway. I never learned to read sheet music, I just play by ear, but I can show you what I do know."

"Cool." Wasps circled their food wrappers, so Jed began gathering the rubbish to put into bags on the ATV. "Hey you too, time to get moving. I'll clean this up. Who wants to go pick berries for Aunt Kari?"

As expected, Lisa and Aaron went hunting for wild strawberries growing on the rocky hillside beside them. Tiny and succulent, they were a favorite of Kari's, so she would make strawberry tarts for them whenever they could bring back a container.

Chloe stayed behind and helped Jed pick up the remains from their late lunch. When the kids removed all signs of their presence, Jed shucked his T-shirt, ran to the water, and jumped in.

"C'mon, Chloe—one more swim, and then we'll be heading back home." Jed dove underneath the water to perform a handstand, his muscular legs rising straight and high in the air. He resurfaced and taunted her to join him. "C'mon, Chloe—bet you can't do a handstand like that."

"Watch me." Chloe debated removing her shirt, then decided against it. She ran into the water and dived in, trying to copy Jed. Her legs came up, one at a time, but quickly toppled over.

Jed chuckled. "Not as easy as it looks, is it? Get a solid footing for your hands, then keep your legs together and raise them."

Chloe dove again and tried to hang onto a large rock, this time getting both legs raised together but toppling before reaching the vertical stance.

"Try it again, Chloe. This time I'll help you get your legs straight up, then let you balance on your own."

Chloe dove again, kept her legs together, and slowly raised them out of the water. She felt Jed's hands grasp her calves and pull them perpendicular. Chloe could hear him telling her to concentrate, and then he loosened his hold. For probably five seconds, she remained in a perfect position, then toppled again. She resurfaced, her chest heaving for breath. "That was better. Let's try it again."

With Jed helping her, Chloe accomplished three more handstands before trying one entirely on her own. Although she was only up a handful of seconds, she was proud of herself.

"Your legs were together but slanted, not straight up and down, but you're getting the hang of it. Want to try again?"

"No thanks, I'm done for today. It's harder than it looks. Thanks, Jed." Chloe swiped the water from her face, then pulled her hair back behind her ears and wrung the water out. She glanced at Jed, who was staring at her lips before turning quickly to shore. His serious expression sent a shiver of attraction through her.

As Chloe followed him, Jed grabbed her towel, tossed it at her, and then headed back to lay on his towel to dry in the sun. She dried herself quickly, then threw it right back at him, hitting him squarely on the back of the head.

"You really want to do this?" Jed's eyes were sparkling as he dared her to continue. "If you want your towel, you'll have to fight me for it."

Chloe kept her eyes glued on his and slowly approached him, then lunged to grab the towel from his football hold. She tripped and fell into Jed. His arms went to steady her as the towel dropped to the beach. Chloe giggled and lunged to retrieve it.

"No fair, that's cheating. You can't fake an accident and grab it. You're supposed to fight me for it."

"Girls have to do what they have to do. I'd never be able to wrestle you for it." Chloe laughed as she moved away from him and laid her towel on the beach not far away. She laid down on her side, with her head in her hand, watching him settle on his towel. Sitting behind him on the ATV and holding onto his waist had triggered new feelings inside of her. Was he feeling the same way?

Jed turned to face her, then reached out and ran his hand over her wet hair before placing a loose strand behind her ear. "You know, for a girl, you're not half bad. I might even call you cute."

Chloe felt her face flush at his compliment, but before she could muster a reply, Aaron and Lisa were back with their container of strawberries, which they placed between her and Jed before jumping in for a final swim.

CHAPTER 4 - THE ARMSTRONGS

Mark Armstrong studied his wife sleeping in her armchair. Gwen appeared so tired. He hoped he'd done the right thing by moving them to his friend Thomas' Safe Haven. Leaving Seattle was easier than he'd thought it'd be. Gwen had been born and raised there, while Mark joined her after they married. That was thirty-five years ago.

More than a lifetime for some.

Mark tapped her shoulder. "Honey, let's go to bed. Come on." He leaned forward and put his hands underneath her arms to help her up. "You can sleep in tomorrow. No more early days for you."

Gwen blinked her eyes open, slowly becoming aware of her new surroundings. "Yes, it's been quite the week. Packing up the basics then traveling for two days almost did me in. You're right, Mark. This move has been a good idea." Gwen yawned and stretched. "No more early mornings. No more frantic phone calls. No more—" Her breath hitched as the familiar pain swept through her.

Mark knew what she felt because he felt it too. Same as his mind knew what'd she been about to say—*no more Sally.*

Gwen pushed Mark's helping hands aside. "I can get up on my own, Mark. I'm not dead yet."

"Getting feisty, are you? Glad to see it. I'm going to turn off the heatilator on the fireplace and the lights. Then I'll be right behind you." Mark watched his wife disappear down the hallway, one hand on the wall to help her manage walking with her sore knee.

Mark glanced about the living room, happy to see that only a few boxes were left to unpack. Except for a beautifully framed portrait taken on their thirtieth-anniversary cruise, there were no pictures displayed yet, and he wondered if there ever would be. Perhaps they could look for scenery pictures to adorn their walls. There must be a good selection of gorgeous ones depicting the beautiful west coast and the mountainous peaks surrounding them. They could both take comfort in that.

Mark heard Gwen preparing for bed and gave her time to get settled. He poured them each a glass of water and brought it to their bedside tables. "Here you go, my love. Did you take your pills?"

"Yes. Did you?"

"In a minute, once I brush my teeth." He took metoprolol at night to calm his racing heart and a high blood pressure pill in the morning. All preventative, the doctors declared. He was lucky. He'd always been mentally as well as physically healthy and active. Thank God. Because watching his wife slowly losing her zest for life had been agonizing. Gwen refused his reassurances that she had done everything she could. It would take time, but he knew their broken hearts *would* heal.

Sliding into bed beside his wife, he laid on his side and watched his wife sleeping. Since Sally died a year ago, Gwen didn't bother coloring her hair anymore. The salt and pepper effect on her was still attractive to him, drawing attention to her deep brown eyes. Gwen appeared at peace in sleep, the crow's feet around her eyes and the lines around her mouth diminished. One day she'd relax again. If he accomplished nothing else for the rest of his life, he would be satisfied to see her greet each day with enthusiasm.

Mark flipped on his back and put his hand underneath his head. Sleep didn't come so quickly for him anymore, but at least now he could rest. Mark could close his eyes and daydream until slumber crept in and dulled his senses. Smiling, he remembered the first time he had accompanied his boss, Charlie, on a fishing trip to Bella Bella. Almost twenty years ago now. It had been a heck of a party. Six guys and two boats with a whole week to abandon the cares of the world.

Pacific King Adventure Lodge in St. John's Harbor was a luxurious, floating resort for the wealthy just outside of Bella Bella. Although the clientele could imagine they were roughing it in the great outdoors, in truth, the grand forty-two suite accommodations offered the very best of life in a remote location. From whale watching, halibut, or King Salmon fishing to scuba diving or simply relaxing in the rustic logged wall living areas, the outside world couldn't reach them. For those who preferred to stay on land, guided ATV tours were available to explore the mountainous terrain around Bella Bella and further east to Bella Coola and the Tweedsmuir Provincial Park.

When Charlie asked Mark to join them as the lead mechanic on the expedition, he jumped at the chance. He'd be bringing in the new 36' Boston Whaler with three 350 HP Furados for their most important corporate buyer while they took a seaplane into the fishing resort. Every second year since 2010, the Sound IT conglomerate had purchased a similar boat for their executives to escape and re-energize themselves. This benefit had proven to be an exceptional draw for new recruits. Every summer, they would book time for their most valued employees to stay in one of the several lodges on the West Coast and Haida Gwaii. Then they would arrange for the boats to be brought back down to Seattle to enjoy there.

After the first few trips, however, Mark opted out of accompanying the hotshots. He'd bring up a boat, enjoying the luxury of its leather armchair while maneuvering with speed and ease. Mark would spend a day or two until everyone was comfortable running them, then escape to Bella Coola and rent a cabin for three or four days. Mark was on the ocean so often that he'd head towards the mountainous peaks inland whenever he had the chance. That's where he met Thomas, who guided him on ATV tours and eventually became a trusted friend. A friend who had recommended Safe Haven.

Funny how life goes. You never know when you'll meet someone who will change your life—maybe not immediately, but somewhere down the line. You just hoped the change would be a positive one. He'd bet his last dollar that Gwen would trade everything she owned to have resisted befriending one of her patients named Doug.

DOUG HAD COME into their lives twelve years ago. He was twenty-three when Gwen took him on as a client through a court rehabilitation order. Still sporting a short military cut, his dark brown hair and tiger eyes attracted attention. A beguiling, lopsided grin revealed even white teeth, cementing the impression that he was a dependable man.

As a soldier decorated for bravery while in Iraq, Doug came home a hero on his second tour. Only he couldn't accept the hypocrisy the honor bestowed upon him. Less than a year after Doug left the military, he was in trouble.

Gwen had worked with veterans before, and his appearance had coaxed her into accepting his request for therapy to help him readjust to civilian life. Mark knew that Gwen often wondered why she'd let herself fall for Doug's charms. But as the young veteran told his story, Gwen believed she could make a difference in his life. Later, she thought she should've known better.

Like many soldiers, Doug didn't hesitate to kill the enemy, no matter who they portrayed themselves to be. He'd protect his fellow troopers at all costs. Most of the time, it had been a good decision, one that otherwise would have killed one of his own. Other times, the victim's nervousness wasn't because they were a threat. They were just plain scared, and in the split-second Doug had to decide, he made mistakes. Classified as collateral damage, Doug still had trouble accepting their needless deaths at his hand.

Once stateside, the military asked him to speak to high schools and colleges throughout his home state of Washington to enlist recruits. Looking at the young faces who only saw the adventure of travel or the pride of serving their country put a quick end to that career. His resignation stated post-traumatic stress complications, which the military doctor agreed could be the source of his supposedly uncontrolled anxiety.

When Doug returned home, his parents were proud of him, always bragging to their neighbors or relatives that their son came home with a medal. He couldn't tell his parents what it was really like in a foreign land, couldn't tell them how scared every last one of them was before going on deployment. That wouldn't fit with their ideal of a brave American soldier.

After resigning from the recruitment posting, he could see the disappointment on his parents' faces. Doug tried to justify his need for a joint to cope with the anxieties his service had caused. Eventually, he'd told his parents everything.

One day, Doug packed his duffle bag, said goodbye to his parents, and hit the road. Hitchhiking from Spokane to Seattle, he met several ex-militaries along the way. Sometimes at an American Legion Hall, he'd drink beer and have dinner, then play pool. Others there were wanderers like himself. Around for a few days, then gone. Doug was fortunate that he had a reasonably good-sized bank account and could choose how and when he traveled. He usually stayed a week or two at a cheap motel, then moved on.

Ever since Doug left his hometown, he refused to take his antianxiety medication. He preferred to buy an ounce of weed and roll himself and friends a joint to mellow out. However, six months later, he found himself down to his last hundred dollars. No more motels now. He found himself on the street with other men in the same predicament. Soon, he found different ways to make money to survive. His favorite was hustling pool. Unfortunately, it often led to being involved in a fight outside the establishment and his winnings stolen.

The State police booked Doug for the second time for impaired and disorderly. When the judge reviewed his file, he gave the young man a chance. Rehabilitation for six months or jail. A no-brainer for Doug. He contacted the

Legion on Alaska Street, securing a studio suite in a veteran's re-purposed garage. Then he researched his options. Go the military route or community mental health centers. After a phone call home, he arranged for local treatment through an outreach program. He found a compassionate listener and reasonable rates his parents could afford with Gwen Armstrong.

FUNNY HOW LIFE GOES. Although Gwen had a kind heart, she wasn't blind to people's tendencies to lie not only to others but to themselves. She was observant and was seldom wrong in her assessment of people. It was like Gwen had a bullshit detector during her new client reviews. Within two visits max, she could see whether she'd be able to help her patient. Mark admired and trusted her intuition and seldom worried about her safety. If she wasn't comfortable, she passed them on to another counselor. Some clients dealt well with women, while others lied through their teeth to get their approval.

Either Gwen's bullshit detector malfunctioned, or Doug changed drastically. Mark didn't know which. All he knew was by the end of the six months, his wife had failed to see the danger signs, and their daughter had fallen in love with Doug and disappeared.

Sally was nineteen. She was an adult, technically. But so naïve, so trusting. She was in her first year at Seattle Central College. Inquisitive and bright, she took various courses the first year to see where she'd *'find herself.'* It turns out she fell in love with communications and theater. Her choice hadn't surprised them. She'd always been somewhat of an emotional drama queen with her tall, blonde, and voluptuous figure. When Sally met Doug at a community fundraising event that Gwen suggested he might enjoy, the attraction was instant.

Gwen tried to talk to her daughter. Without specifics, she explained the problems that some ex-military had with PTSD. But when pressed, she had to admit that Doug had a stable background with supportive parents. With the right help, he could have a promising future ahead of him. That's all it took for Sally.

She was going to save him. Sally was going to help him be the healthiest and best person for her future too.

Mark and Gwen had discussed this many, endless times. It was nothing short of tragic what was happening to many young people lately. Failure to succeed on the first or second try wasn't in their vocabulary. The luckier ones went home to their families, regrouped, and continued forward. Others found a way to hide their disappointment with booze or drugs and a myriad of excuses.

For Doug and Sally, it started with weed. When financial pressures grew too hard for them to handle, Doug became involved in distribution. From the odd phone call from Sally, life was good. They lived in a one-bedroom suite on East Olive Way. It was close enough to the Seattle Central College for Sally to have attended if she hadn't screwed up. Being caught trying to sell weed to a sophomore on campus had triggered Sally's expulsion. They lost track of them for a long, agonizing year. The next time they had heard from Sally was from a phone call from a police station.

Sally repeated her excuse that it was all a mistake. They insisted they weren't involved with selling coke. They just happened to be at a party where drugs were. When a noise complaint brought a police raid, they were arrested. Angry that her parents also refused to bail Doug out, Sally was belligerent and antsy. Stress became a heavy burden as their daughter paced the floor while confined at home with an ankle monitor until her court date.

That was the first time. Mark and Gwen had cashed in almost half of their 401(k) to pay for a lawyer. However, it was Sally's first offense, and if it kept her out of jail, then it was worth it. Once Sally realized how close to incarceration she was, it seemed to have woken her up. She followed the strict rules of her probation, albeit begrudgingly.

Six months later, when Doug was released, Sally was gone again. So much for learning her lesson. For the next few years, their only contact with her was short text messages with pictures of a revolving door of residences. She and Doug were traveling on a route from Washington to California, selling medical office supplies. From the clothes they wore, they were good with their sales pitches. Occasionally, Gwen and Mark would receive pictures of them were wearing the latest fashions while dining at waterfront restaurants.

Mark and Gwen were now parents on a '*need to know*' basis. Sally and Doug ignored any questions about where they were living, when they'd come back home, or who to contact in case of an emergency. It was a one-way communication street. It took them a long time to stop worrying every minute of the day. As long as the occasional text and photo came through, they had to be content that their daughter looked healthy and happy.

They had two choices. Either accept it and hope for the best or spend the rest of their lives worrying and trying to fix someone who didn't want their help. So, they chose hope.

THE SMELL of bacon frying awakened Mark, which was very unusual. Typically, he'd always been the early riser, but since he retired, things were slowly changing. Last night, he'd had trouble shutting down his brain. Although he wouldn't admit he'd been worrying, he conceded to reviewing his life. He wanted to focus on the present and enjoy each day. Nothing would change if they couldn't bury their past regrets.

He threw on his bathrobe and went into the kitchen, sneaking up behind his wife and hugging her. "Smells great, honey. Can I help?"

"Pour yourself a coffee. I was just waiting for you to get up before I cooked your eggs. How many today? Two or three?"

"Better make it three. Thomas and I are going to his grandparents' farm to cut down old fruit trees. Their wood will be good for smoking meat and fish in the fall. When we get back, we'll continue chopping wood. We need to have at least ten cords for the winter. I have to do my share. And once I start, I don't like to stop and eat."

"I know. Better drink lots of water then. You aren't a young man anymore. You have to be careful."

"Don't worry. Thomas makes sure we take breaks often. I don't know if he does that with the other guys, but he does when we're together. Sonja is supposed to drop by sometime this afternoon, and she usually brings us a snack."

"Vera and I are going into town to pick up as many cases as we can get for canning. Both quart and pints." Gwen put down their breakfast plates, then took the buttered toast from the oven.

"It's been a long time since I've done any of that, but I'll follow Vera's guidance. She's also ordered a vacuum packer from Amazon for things we'll freeze. I'd rather do that than bend over gardening. It will keep me busy."

Mark bit into a thick strip of home-cured bacon and rolled his eyes in appreciation. "I don't know if it's the fresh air or the fresh food, but everything tastes so darn good here. How do you like it so far? Are you getting along with the ladies?"

"I am. Everyone seems friendly without overdoing it. It's good to have something different to focus on in our life. I wasn't sure how I'd like retirement, not having a job to go to every day. Although I have to admit, I don't miss listening to other people's problems. Been there, done that."

"Yup. It's time for us to concentrate on what *we* want to do." Mark sopped the remainder of his egg yolks with the thick homemade bread they had bought in town, then pushed his plate away. Mark's left eyebrow rose. "Do you have anything planned for tomorrow?"

"Nothing in particular. Unpack boxes or join up again with Vera."

"How about if the two of us get away and explore? You haven't seen much except for town. I'd like to take you to Odegaard Falls. It's only an hour and a half from here. What do you think?" Mark left the table and went to grab a light sweatshirt and gloves.

"Sounds good to me. I'll pack us a lunch and drinks in the cooler."

Mark watched Gwen approach him with a bright smile and anticipation in her eyes. She hugged him tightly and kissed his cheek.

He lowered his head and nuzzled her neck. "We're going to have fun exploring and doing things we've put off for years. You'll see. I may even start making that cedar-strip canoe I've dreamed of."

Gwen chuckled as she punched his arm. "Anything's possible, sweetheart. Maybe I'll learn something new too."

"I remember when we first started going out, you'd always have charcoal and sketching paper whenever we went for a picnic. You used to be pretty good at it, but you never kept it up after you started working full-time. Ever thought of doing that again?"

"No. I wouldn't have a clue where to start. I think those days are long gone, but who knows?"

"Never say never, Gwen. Keep your eyes open for something that strikes your interest. Winters are long here. We'll need to find a hobby or learn how to play cards." Mark slapped his cap on and opened the door. "Think about it." He blew her a kiss and walked to the main lodge.

GWEN CLEARED the table and cleaned her kitchen, then poured herself another cup of coffee. She took a tablet of paper and started calculating. She and Mark couldn't deny the facts. Since early in their marriage, the 401(k)s that both had contributed to no longer existed. Gwen tapped her fingers against her temple as she tried to assemble her thoughts.

Moving here had been a wise decision.

Being reminded of how their life was in Seattle after Sally died was dragging them both down. Gwen had given her notice and taken early retirement at 62. After a month's leave, Mark had returned to work at Shoreline Motors, but he couldn't concentrate on his job and gave his notice too.

When Mark and Gwen finally faced the facts eight months later, they knew if they were going to survive the death of their daughter, the couple needed to find a new home. Somewhere far from the prying questions of well-intentioned colleagues and friends. Somewhere they could escape the busy city life. Retirement was a double-edged sword. True, it gave them the solitude and privacy they needed right now. But without their full income, they couldn't afford their mortgage and strata fees anymore. Most of their savings were gone, and before their back was to the wall, it was time to sell.

Mark and Gwen agonized over the decisions they had made over the past dozen years. The attempts they made to save Sally from her life of addiction. Now they went over each episode, second-guessing if another way would've brought better results. Yes, their financial situation wasn't what they had hoped to have when they planned to retire. But had there really been another choice that they could've accepted? In their minds and hearts, there wasn't. They could rest easy that they did everything they could. Money was money. Nice to have, but it didn't buy happiness. If they wanted to find happiness again, they needed to take steps to find it, and it wouldn't be in Seattle.

Gwen dropped her pencil and went to the fridge, and poured herself a glass of orange juice. She sat in the living room, looking at the mountains just beyond their community. Gwen sipped her juice and zoned out while she reviewed why they had moved up here. She rued the day she ever took Doug on as a client. Maybe it would've happened anyway, but in her mind, it was Doug's influence that had started her daughter down a torturous path. When Sally's first brush with the law happened, she was still in college, Gwen was shocked. Holding six ounces of weed and selling it to her fellow students? She was raised with better morals than that. A first-time offense and a good lawyer resulted in probation and mandatory therapy.

At first, Gwen had tried the cheaper option of outpatient rehab for her daughter, believing with her background and connections, Sally would get the support she needed to turn her life around. The trouble was Doug. Even with a restraining order, he found a way to appear in Sally's life. Sometimes it was at the grocery store or standing outside the clinic after a session. Even if he didn't approach Sally, it was enough to trigger anxiety attacks, which Sally tried to quell with liquor. Then one day, Sally was gone. And the waiting to see her daughter started again.

The next time Sally reached out was years later and from a hospital bed. She had OD'd, though luckily, the ambulance was nearby and able to resuscitate with naloxone. Frightened from the experience, Sally agreed to attend an inpatient rehab for sixty days. She responded well after the initial detox from heroin. When she came home that time, Sally began an outpatient program and was proud of her success. She got a job at a grocery store and started paying rent at home.

The sixty-thousand-dollar withdrawal from their pension fund hurt, but it felt worth it to have their daughter healthy and with them again.

Almost a year later, Sally moved into a small one-bedroom apartment near Fry's Grocery. She was so excited about her progress and her future. She'd come for dinner once a week and tell them about her new life, happy that her parents were proud of her again. But when the economy took a nosedive, she was laid off from work. She applied for Employment Insurance, but anxiety soon filled her empty days.

When Sally missed her weekly dinner with no excuse, Gwen hoped it wasn't anything serious. However, after a week of leaving messages begging Sally to call, they went to her apartment to check on her. They asked for a wellness inspection, and the landlady was kind enough to let them peek inside. The inside was a mess, and when they went to her closet, it confirmed their worst fears. Most of her things were gone. Gwen honestly wondered if she'd have a heart attack. Her heart literally felt like it was breaking. She couldn't catch her breath, and tremors traveled through her from head to toe.

Thank God for Mark. Gwen took a leave from work for a month while she recuperated from a bout of depression. Mark took the first week off, too, hoping he'd be able to encourage Gwen not to see Sally's failure as a reflection on them. It was *her* disease, *her* problem to solve. They had done everything that was in their power to help.

Gwen knew all the reasons rehabilitations failed. Intellectually, she knew they had no power to help their daughter unless she was committed to it. Eventually, Mark and Gwen accepted it as truth and swore they wouldn't step in anymore. If they saw their daughter again, if Sally wanted help again, she'd have to take all the steps independently. They wouldn't turn her away, but they wouldn't make it easy for her either.

Convinced this was the right way to handle it, they concentrated on making their own lives happier. They bought a second-hand boat that needed work and threw themselves into the project, eventually touring the sound and the Strait of Juan de Fuca. Life was good. Lonely, if they let themselves think as parents, but good.

And true to form, a few years later, they received texts and the odd picture of their daughter. It stirred hope in their hearts and a longing to see Sally once more. They tried hard not to get excited. Nevertheless, there was anticipation in their lives again.

Sally had aged. Her life experiences had caught up with her. She was skin and bones, and her eyes appeared haunted, her smile forced. She was sharing an apartment with women she worked with at Denny's. But she was reaching out. Thank God.

Hope is a strange emotion. It's a beautiful thing when it blooms. But when hope fades, when it begins to wither, it strikes fear deep inside until it transforms into despair. Then it strips the goodness from your life. Life becomes gray.

That's how both Gwen and Mark felt when they received a call of Sally's arrest. An outstanding warrant for failure to appear on a prostitution charge followed by a drug possession with intent to distribute meant she probably wouldn't be out of jail for long.

They were in shock. Mark and Gwen were afraid to go and see Sally. For hours after her call, Gwen had held her husband as he sobbed in disappointment. She'd never seen Mark collapse like that before. This time she was the strong one who called the lawyer they had used several years prior.

Mr. Woods strongly advised that they leave Sally in custody until her hearing, a form of 'scared straight.' Gwen and Mark agreed with a heavy heart. After several meetings with Sally, the lawyer arranged another meeting with Gwen and Mark and outlined a proposal he wanted to offer the prosecution. Another sixty-day rehab in central Washington, near Quincy. A rural setting, back to nature and healthy living, away from city life. And two-year probation to follow. Mr. Woods believed a tough-love response this time might be the way to go. He suggested they not visit Sally until she'd been treated at Blue Sky Refuge for at least a month, or more depending on her therapists' advice. Once again, after much soul searching, they agreed.

How many times can a heart break? How many times does a parent try to help? For Mark and Gwen, it was for as long as there was hope. As embarrassing as it was for Gwen, they signed up for counseling to help them deal with their problem. If they couldn't find peace for the two of them, Sally wouldn't be the only casualty of drug use. She'd destroy their marriage too.

By the time Sally finished her stint at rehab, she was once again the bright-eyed daughter they hoped would return. She chose to stay in Quincy and attend an outpatient program through the Blue Sky Refuge. Gwen and Mark texted weekly with Sally and encouraged her progress. With the cost of treatment and probably future financial support for Sally, they decided to sell their house and buy a small condominium. What was the point of a big family home for two people? There were no grandchildren in the picture, no need for a yard anymore. So, Gwen and Mark downsized.

Life was peaceful for the next few years. The program worked well, and hope straggled up from the wreckage of their life, searching for light. They shared a cautious optimism that the worst was over. Sally had grown up. Mark had moved up in his department at Shoreline Motors. He assisted their elite boating customers, often moving their boats from Seattle to Victoria or Vancouver and other locations. Gwen reduced her work week to three days a week, then joined a ladies' outdoor club, often hiking or kayaking. They all concentrated on learning how to enjoy the good things in life again.

Ingrained in Gwen's memory forever was the Saturday morning when she and Mark were enjoying coffee on their balcony, the view of the coastal mountains lifting their spirits. The doorbell rang, and when Mark raised his eyebrow,

Gwen spread her hands out. "I don't know. I'm not expecting anyone. Maybe Joe wants to go golfing."

The doorbell rang again, and Mark got up to answer it. Gwen could hear a deep voice mumbling something, then her husband mumbling. The door closed.

"Gwen? Honey? You need to come in here."

"I'm sure you can make your own lunch for golf, dear."

"Gwen. It isn't about golf." Mark's voice trembled as he looked at his wife sitting outside, sipping her coffee.

Gwen turned and looked closer at her husband through the screened patio door. She put her mug down quickly and went inside. "What? What's wrong? Is it Sally?"

Whenever something terrible happened, Sally was usually behind it.

"She's gone, Gwen. When her neighbor visited this morning, he found her sitting on her sofa with a book on her lap. It looks like she fell asleep and died."

"What the hell? How? Why?" Gwen collapsed to her knees on the floor, her mouth opened in shock. She ran her hands over her cheeks, then over her lips. "I don't believe this. She didn't have heart problems. Was it drugs?"

"Nobody knows yet. An autopsy will tell. Her neighbor said she liked to take a valium or something like that to relax at night and read a book. The police wonder if it was something legitimate or if it was a street drug laced with fentanyl. There's been a lot of that happening around the state. The ambulance brought her to the morgue in Quincy."

"My God. My God. Now, what do we do?" Gwen trembled as tears came to her eyes.

"Pack an overnight bag. We'll drive over there. Then, we'll visit Sally's apartment and talk to her neighbor. Maybe we can find out more. Do you know who her doctor is?"

"No. I just know the doctors at Blue Sky. But I can text them and ask them for the information. I don't want to talk to them, Mark. I simply can't tell them what's happened."

"You don't need to, honey. Just text the basics and tell them you aren't accepting calls right now but need the information texted back to you."

Mark had sat beside her and held her in his arms, stroking her soft hair gently. When her trembling subsided, he'd helped her to her feet and kissed her, then held her hand as he'd led her into the bedroom to pack and see their daughter one final time.

A KNOCK at the door startled Gwen and interrupted her reverie. Her heart quickened in alarm until she glanced at her watch and saw the time. Darn, she was still in her housecoat, and her new friend was there.

"Hi, Vera. I'm sorry-I must have dozed off in my chair. I haven't been sleeping well."

"Not to worry. You've been so busy that it isn't surprising you're tired." Vera put a hand on Gwen's shoulder compassionately. "Would you rather stay home? We can always shop tomorrow if you want."

"No, please—I'd like to go out. Can you wait for me to get ready? Ten minutes tops."

Gwen felt Vera's concern and rushed to reassure her. She masked her fatigue, putting a lilt into her voice. "Honestly, I'm fine, and going out for a while will perk me up."

"Are you sure? We can postpone the trip for another day. There's no rush."

"I know, but I was looking forward to your company and

seeing the town. There's iced tea in the fridge. Please help yourself while I get ready, ok? I won't be long, I promise."

"Alright. Don't panic. We have lots of time. Maybe we'll stop and have coffee in town, make an afternoon of it. We're in no hurry."

Gwen smiled. "Sounds great. Back in a minute." She saw the notepad and pencil on the table, so she quickly picked them up and put them in a drawer. The budget would have to wait for another day. Next time she wouldn't let herself go down memory lane. The past was behind her, and there was no use visiting it.

Right now, she needed a friend more than she needed to focus on finances. Gwen favored her left knee as she hurried down the hallway to her bedroom to change and put on a little makeup.

CHAPTER 5 - THE DEVRIES

B en Devries automatically pushed on his right hip and
arched his back to ease the strain he always suffered
when standing on his feet too long. Vera gave him a sidelong
glance but didn't say a word. It wouldn't have helped
anyway, and she knew it. The day he couldn't haul in his
supplies and do his own butchering would be the day he'd
put his knives away for good.

"Is the rest going to be processed for ground pork?" Vera
asked.

"Yes. Not today, though. I'll put the scraps into the walk-
in cooler and tackle that tomorrow. Do you need a hand
with packaging the rest of those chops?"

"No, it won't take me long. Four to a pack, right?"

"Yup. It's the most convenient size. It will make two
meals for couples, and the families can take a pack or two to
feed themselves. I've made the roasts around three pounds
too so that everyone can choose what suits them. You don't
need to vacuum pack the soup bones. Just put them in
plastic bags along with the rest of the meat, then into the
walk-in freezer. Pork goes on the left." Ben arched his back

again and sighed. "Won't be long before we're too old for this, Vera."

"That's why we must teach the younger ones how to do these jobs. We can still supervise, make sure all aspects of organic gardening and correct food preservation is passed onto the next generation." Vera shooed him out of her way. "Why don't you head home and relax? I'll finish this job and the clean-up within an hour and follow you."

Ben nodded and made his way out of the working cooler. Tomorrow he'd season the hind legs from the eight pigs they butchered this week and start the smoking process. Thomas promised to bring in applewood from his grandparents' farm, which would enhance the flavor.

It wouldn't be long that they would start butchering a couple of cows, then processing the yield from the hunting and fishing season. From May to the end of September was the most active months for survivalists to get ready, and no matter what these people called themselves, that's what they were. Oh, it was true that some families had outside jobs to bring cash income to Safe Haven, but when push came to shove, he was sure that they would look after their own first.

Ben knew he had to make a decision soon about replacing Vera at his side. She needed to start the drying and preserving of fruit and vegetables. When it was just the two of them, they managed to do everything together, but now that there was a whole community to plan and provide for, they needed to organize things differently. This evening was the bi-weekly meeting at the main lodge, where everyone was required to attend. He'd bring up the subject then. As head of this department, if no one volunteered, he could name the person he thought was best suited. He hoped it would be Ray. Strong and energetic, he had an easy-going personality that would complement Ben's work ethic. He went to the deep metal sink, washed his hands thoroughly, dried them, and then used sanitizer.

Ben returned home and sat on his porch, taking a rest before going inside. His gaze roved the land that he watched take shape and grow. It was a miniature village now, well planned and over half full. Matt, Thomas, and Ray should be proud of what they accomplished here.

Intentional Living Matt called it. Apparently, these communities were more successful if various groups lived in them, old and young, homebodies, and outside workers. Everyone worked in one way or another to help their village sustain themselves and have a better lifestyle. It reminded him of a new and improved Hippie lifestyle from the sixties and seventies. Minus the drugs and promiscuity, of course.

At first, when Vera mentioned joining the complex, Ben had resisted. He wasn't a particularly religious man, although he did believe in God and karma. The rest seemed to be much too open for interpretation. But a year after being hired by Matt, he had a better vision of what they had hoped to accomplish, and he agreed to join.

Although Ben was skeptical of Matt's fears for Washington State, he couldn't begrudge him the right to prepare for the worst—as long as he didn't push his beliefs on the rest of them. Climate change was no joke, but time would tell if Matt's predictions were warranted. Living here on land that once belonged to his grandfather would improve those impacted by the chaos of natural and manmade catastrophes if it should come to that.

He and Vera should be retired, but they were workaholics, and they'd worked all of their lives. What would they do with long days and nothing to do? They'd worked up and down the west coast of B.C. in Rivers and Bute Inlet, all the way up into the Douglas Channel. Unfortunately, the work was sporadic. Being a camp cook for gypo outfits meant layoffs for snow or fire season or a downturn in the economy. They usually broke even from year to year, saving for a few years, then using it all up in a bad year.

By joining Safe Haven, they wouldn't have to pay rent, only utilities, as long as they looked after food sustainability. Now their government pensions would be enough to make their senior years more comfortable.

Looking down at his hands, he opened the brown jar of cream and smoothed a little on each finger. Then he rubbed each finger, massaging the knuckles, then stretching them forward and backward to keep them limber. Arthritis was a bitch, he acknowledged, but he had found a natural remedy that worked better than all the ointments and pills he'd tried in the stores. He'd always thought cannabis cream was a hoax and that he'd never try it. But when a friend had given him the tail end of his jar to try, he was surprised at how quickly he felt the difference.

At first, Ben used it two to three times a day. Now he only used it when his arthritis flared up, especially after a hard day of working in a cooler. The cold seemed to penetrate and seize his joints until he couldn't make a fist. Ben could grip his knives tightly now and make a fist anytime he needed to. He didn't drop things anymore either, so Ben was a believer and recommended it to anyone having problems with their joints. Rubbing another dab of cream into the tendons on the inside of his wrist helped too. Growing old wasn't for the faint of heart, and he was going to fight it every step of the way.

Closing his eyes, Ben laid his head back, breathing in the scents of life in their community. The smell of pastures, a distant whiff of the barns and sheds, then a breeze from the nearby hillside of cedar and pine. The aroma of cinnamon and apples from Kari's open door. Life was good.

VERA FINISHED HER JOB, then cleaned the butcher's block, floor, and sink before taking the pail of offal into the freezer. Ben could dispose the several buckets of organic refuse into the dumpsite a few miles away. Ray had taken the little Kubota over last week and dug a four-foot hole. He'd also brought several truckloads of sawdust, then left a dozen bags of lime to use to cover each layer. Everything had to be planned and prepped before starting a project like butchering. And nobody could plan better than Ben.

As Vera made her way back home, she saw Ben sitting on the porch waiting for her, his ball cap tipped over his eyes and his feet propped up on the railing. What a sweetheart. He was truly the other half of her. Without him, she didn't know what she'd do. They knew each other so well that talk wasn't always necessary. They were attuned to each other's moods as well as their needs, often anticipating what needed to happen next.

As she drew closer, he didn't stand to greet her as he usually did. Concerned, she skipped quickly across the yard and up the steps.

"Honey?" Vera rubbed his forearm gently and felt him jerk and straighten in his chair. "Caught you snoozing, didn't I?"

"You did alright." Ben yawned. "Would you like to sit outside for a while? I'll go get us some iced tea."

"Yes, that would be great. Take a look in the cupboard by the fridge. I think there are still muffins in there. That would hit the spot right now."

Vera sat, relieved yet a little saddened to see her strong, energetic husband snoozing in the chair. He continued to work like a horse, yet he was done for the day when he stopped now. She was fine with that—it was time to enjoy life more at their age.

She knew he also worried about her now and then. When preserving started, she'd have long days too. Thank God for electric utensils. Time-consuming jobs such as chopping, dicing, and pureeing were done in a quarter of the time it used to take. They'd be using the large kitchen in the main lodge when it came to harvest and processing. Three pressure cookers would also make short work of the canning ritual.

The screen door squeaked open with a kick from Ben. Each hand-carried an iced tea, with a bread plate balanced on top, holding a blueberry muffin.

"You haven't lost your touch. You can still balance a handful of food." Vera reached for her snack and watched her husband make himself comfortable again. "I like the pace we've set for ourselves here. Work in the morning 'til around two, then stop and enjoy the afternoon."

"It's enough. There'll be days we'll have to do more, but Matt made sure to let me know to ask for help if there was too much for us to handle. Part of what makes this place work is not to be shy to ask for a hand, rather than over-doing it."

"I agree. I like the work bees approach. It reminds me of when we were young. My family often got together to help someone out. Then they have a big pot luck dinner afterward. I remember it was a lot of fun. A chance for all of us to visit, keep in touch, and accomplish a project."

"Us too. I had six sets of uncles and aunts. There was always somebody needing something." Ben chuckled at the memory, drawing his hand across his chin. "Didn't take long either, probably because no booze was allowed until everyone got their jobs done."

Vera laughed and sipped her drink. "Same as in our work bees. Otherwise, Dad said, too many mistakes were made, which was probably true. And mistakes cost time and money, both things that were in short supply around the farm we lived on."

"Our lives have gone full circle, haven't they? We were both raised on farms in the Peace River district, and now we're back living on one."

"That's fine for me. I'm happier here than I'd be if we lived in an apartment in town. Much happier." Vera took a bite of her blueberry muffin glazed with sweet lemon, then licked her lips. "Kari is quite the cook. And apparently, Nathan's sister-in-law is another awesome cook who publishes cookbooks. I can tell we won't be going hungry here."

Ben nodded. "I'm sure we won't go hungry. By the way, only a few people know that Pete's not in good health. Not even his kids have been told. He has leukemia, the slow-moving kind. They want to change their nutritional diet to organic products and eliminate sugar, beef, and pork to slow the progression."

"That makes total sense now. For his age, I thought Pete was rather sluggish. His wife is the busy one with the children and gardening. Before we start preserving, I'll have to talk to her about anything special we need to do for their family. Thanks for the heads up." Vera patted her husband's arm. "Don't worry. I won't mention this to anyone."

"I know you won't. Pete's doing what he can when he feels up to it. He also wants to concentrate on his dream of publishing a manuscript. He's published in the academic world but had always wanted to delve into writing the great Canadian novel. This opportunity is perfect. He's isolated from the hustle and bustle of city life."

"Everybody has a story, don't they? We've got an interesting bunch here already, and more families are yet to come. I hope it turns out as well as they expected."

"Organization is key, and Matt's certainly good at that. It has a good chance. Don't forget there's a meeting tonight at eight. Maybe we should take a siesta this afternoon?" Ben's eyebrows waggled up and down suggestively.

"Oh, you." Vera slapped her husband's thigh playfully. "Let's see how we feel after our shower." Vera giggled, then picked up the dishes and went inside, her husband following with a silly grin on his face.

MATT KNOCKED his gavel three times on the table. "Glad to see everyone here. This gathering is officially the third board of directors' meeting for our Safe Haven Sanctuary. Jed's going to be my secretary and will take the attendance tonight, July 26. Before we go ahead, if you'd please join me in prayer." He watched the current membership fold their hands and bow their heads, then followed suit.

"Dear Lord in Heaven, please guide Your faithful servants here in their quest to live in harmony and faithfulness to Your laws. Let kindness and a commitment to You and this earth steer us into making mindful decisions so we can make this world a better place. Amen." Matt raised his gaze to his friends and smiled. "Does anybody else have something to add?"

Ray stood, clasped his hands, and bowed his head. "I do. Thank you, Lord, for watching over Nathan, Mike, and me when we were stupid enough to build a fire. We were blessed not to have caused a forest fire or hurt anyone. I've apologized to You many times since, as well as to the members of this community. I want to thank everyone for your forgiveness. This mistake will never happen again. Amen."

A murmur of thanks and amens filled the room. Matt knew that everything that needed to be said about that matter had been addressed. Time to move on.

"Go ahead and make this official, Jed. Make a roll call." As Matt watched him call out the names and mark them present, he felt a deep sense of contentment. So far, things have been going very well.

"The notice board reminded members to give an outline of what we've accomplished since our last get-together and any costs involved. Then we need to discuss what we're anticipating for August. Thomas, would you like to start?"

Thomas nodded, then shifted numerous papers before he began reading. "At the beginning of the month, we finished the jungle gym in the playground for the younger kids and put up two tire swings. We bought 2x4s for platforms and railings from Watson's mill for $180.00, the order from Amazon for plastic-coated rungs came in at $85.00. Miscellaneous screws, chains, etc. that I bought at Ace Hardware amounted to a discounted price of $82.00. The total cost was $347.00. Thanks to Nathan for pitching in and giving us a hand."

Thomas looked up and surveyed the group. "Does anyone have any questions?" When no one offered a comment, he continued. "Ok then. We also received our order for 4x4 posts and fencing wire for a padlock for the sheep. The guys have dug most of the holes now, so we'll need to hand mix cement for the bases, then we'll be able to put up the wire. Material costs for the 40x60 enclosure will be close to $1100.00." Thomas looked around the table for any questions or comments. As none popped up, he continued his report.

"In two weeks, we'll have another order in for about the same cost to finish enclosing the vegetable garden. We don't need the deer coming and eating more of our produce. Pete and Vera have already had to re-plant two rows of tomato plants and replant the leaf lettuce. We've put a makeshift netting over it, so hopefully, that will last 'til we get the rest of the fencing supplies."

Laughter mixed with a bit of grumbling permeated the meeting. Deer were beautiful to watch, but they had created problems for the novice gardeners.

"Other than that, Ray and I have been cutting alder for splitting in October. I'd like to mention Mike has joined us, and he's been a great help, hauling the branches out of the way to the burn pile. We'll start work bees to chop and split the firewood and haul it to the woodshed by the end of September. Gardening, harvesting, and fishing will be completed by then, so more bodies should be available to help with that. If anyone wants to join us, let me know." Thomas shuffled his papers back into a neat pile then scanned the crowd, obviously searching for volunteers.

"You've been busy," Matt said, then turned his attention to Matt's quest. "Is anyone, besides Ray and Thomas, available to help with the fence next week? I have Monday free, anyone else?" When Mark held up his hand, he nodded and thanked him. "Jed, please make a note of that and collect Thomas' reports. If anyone else can make time, please don't hesitate to join in—the more, the merrier. And Kari provides delicious lunches and snacks for these work bees. She never gets to bring any leftovers home, that's for sure."

Kari waved. "I'll stay and lend a hand after I deliver the lunch. I'm always good for a gofer if nothing else. Aaron said he'd work with his dad."

"If Aaron's helping, so am I." Jed volunteered as he concentrated on writing his minutes for the board meeting.

"Sounds good. It looks like it will get done quickly with all these volunteers. Ben? What have you to report tonight?"

"Eight pigs butchered this month. I have hinds ready to smoke. I'll be starting that tomorrow. Last month, Ray and Thomas often went out hunting for partridge, so I already have a couple dozen in the freezer. The second batch of chicks arrived a month ago, and they're almost fully feathered. Lisa and Chloe have been feeding and watering them. By the end of September, they'll be ready for butchering for winter. Thomas, Lisa, and Chloe are keeping an eye on the lambs and sheep. We'll butcher the wethers in October, then leave the ewes to grow the herd next year. We also need to check out the livestock at Thomas' parent's place and decide what we take and when. I'm thinking early September. Vera usually helps me, however, I think she'll be too busy in August to be available anymore. So, I'm looking for an assistant for August and September."

"That's true. Vera, Gwen, Denyse, and Pete will be maintaining the garden and harvesting. So, any volunteers for Ben?"

"I can give him a day, maybe two days a week. I wish I could give more, but that's also prime time for my research." Nathan looked apologetic as he lifted his hands. "If I could be in two places at once, I would."

"Everyone does what they can, Nathan, not to worry. These work bees aren't a contest. You'll make up for it later with something else." Matt reassured him, prompting a smile of relief.

"Ben, if you make up a schedule, I'll take two days too. Maybe even three," Mark offered. "I'll do what I can. Although, I hope to be out fishing for halibut off Bella Bella in that time frame too."

Matt looked around at his team. "Thanks, everyone. I know this sounds hectic for the next few months, but this is what we must do to live up to our commitment to live a sustainable life. Our food is grown without pesticides or chemical fertilizers. Our meat is organic and as fresh as you could ever have. And of course, venison and fish are extremely important in our healthy lifestyle. So yes. It will be crazy for August and September." Matt's energy seemed to infuse his members as they listened to his plans.

"Nathan's brother and his wife, Bruce and Erin, will join our Safe Haven for the winter before making a final decision about making the move a permanent one. It's a great time to have an extra set of helpers. Then hunting season will begin, but by November, we should have some lazy days in comparison. We'll have plenty of time to recuperate during the winter." Matt scanned his group and smiled encouragingly.

"*We can do this*. Don't overdo yourself, or it will only cause a delay later. Work smart, not hard—well, not *too* hard!" Matt heard the chuckle around him. Nothing like a little humor to build enthusiasm. "Now, let's hear from Vera."

"Not much to report yet. Gwen and I have started buying our supplies for canning and freezing our vegetables. If anyone has a food allergy or needs low salt or no spice items, we'd like to have that in writing, please, so we can label their products. We will need volunteers in the kitchen, so I'll post a notice and sign-up list on the bulletin board and figure out a schedule. We need to consider re-purposing one of the smaller rooms into a giant pantry so that the bulk of our supplies are stored there. Families can come once a month and pick up what they need. What do you think, Matt?"

"Probably a good idea for a year or two until we have programs that need the space. By then, maybe we'll have added a small building just for that purpose. That's a possibility and a good way to monitor how much we're using too. I'll figure out the cost of shelving and present it at the next meeting. There is limited storage in each home, so that might solve the issue."

"Ok, let's stop for a break. Kari has made her famous brownies, so let's enjoy a beverage and a treat. Then it will be an open discussion."

An hour later, when everyone looked at each other for more information or input, Matt knew it was time to draw the meeting to a close. "The last item I want to bring up is that I've placed an article in the West Coast Intentional Living magazine. I'm hoping to get more applicants that will fit in with our group. Once I narrow down the interested families, I'll do a background check. Then I'll call a special meeting to discuss a shortlist." Matt looked around the room.

"Even though Bruce and Erin will join us in the fall, we still need one more family to enter our community. We've decided to leave one smaller home empty—for adventure charters. In the off-season, extended family members who want to spend time with us will be able to use it. If you know of someone who would be interested, please discuss them with me. Any questions?" Matt perused his membership, then continued.

"Looks like you're all in agreement with what we've discussed." Matt tidied his papers, then smiled at each of the members. "I want to remind all of you that I try to be in my office every afternoon from one to four. There will be a note on the board every morning about where you can find me if I'm not there. Thomas or I am always available by using the walkie-talkie on the wall beside the notice board. I'll usually be around the claim somewhere if an emergency comes up. Now, let's finish the night with a closing prayer. Ray? Will you do the honors?"

Ray stood and asked everyone to join him. "Thank you, Lord, for these friends and family in our Safe Haven. For our good health, the teamwork we've developed, and the lifestyle we are building here. We're grateful for Your continued Guidance. Please help us be the very best we can be. Amen."

A chorus of amens followed. Then, chairs screeched back as the members rose, put the chairs away, and cleaned the dishes. Matt surveyed the contented group he had brought together and added another prayer. *And please send Anna home to us very soon.*

"WHAT DID you think of the meeting, honey?" Vera's hand hooked into the crook of Al's arm as they headed home through the summer's twilight.

"It went well. I saw a hint of panic in Nathan's eyes when he realized he'd have to set aside days for work around here. This group isn't used to working seven days a week—they're used to having weekends off to play. This lifestyle is different. If you plan to work another outside job, you have to make adjustments, at least during the busy times for our community."

"He seems like the decent kind, and he'll find a way. Pete

appeared a little uncomfortable too, but Denyse more than makes up for his short days. Each family is learning as they go along. The load will ease more next year with extra hands."

"True enough. By that time, everyone will be more comfortable in this lifestyle. It isn't like these families knew what would happen here, so it's no wonder they have doubts now and then. Other than the busy harvesting season, the hours are flexible. I think they'll be numerous conversations going on tonight. Like Matt reminded the group, August to the end of September would be the busiest. Now that they're aware of that, they can figure out their schedule for outside work."

"Has Matt talked to you about monetary contributions? I haven't heard anything yet."

"Not much, just that he's working on it and will present it in the fall. It wouldn't surprise me if Matt joined a dental clinic part-time. After all, that was something he loved doing, and it's very lucrative. His accountant keeps track of expenditures, but most of them are one-off items, things that won't pop up again—like the buildings or the fencing. I think he's researching how other intentional communities are navigating that issue. He's smart. He'll make the right decisions."

Ben spread his hands out with a sigh of relief. "It won't make any difference to us. We put in more hours here than anyone except Ray, Kari, Matt, and Thomas. As long as we look after our utilities, that's our contribution. I want to set some money aside from our pensions to contribute if our community hits a tough spot on the road. Can you set up a new bank account for that? Even if it's only a hundred dollars a month."

"Good idea. If the community doesn't need it after a few

ALL FOR FAMILY

years, we can always claw some back, but if there's ever an issue, we can feel that we've also contributed financially." Vera squeezed her husband's arm affectionately. "You're a good man, Charlie Brown."

"Who's this Charlie Brown?" This long-time joke always brought a smile to Ben's face. He tried to be a hard-working, God-fearing man, eternally ready to help his neighbor. And Vera's appreciation and support were his rewards. When she looked up at him with her blue eyes sparkling, nothing mattered except her love.

Ben took her hand and kissed her fingers. No words were needed. Their souls connected in a way that made declarations superfluous. *Thank you, Lord, for this woman.*

CHAPTER 6 - THE HANSENS

At the crack of dawn, Sonja Hansen slipped out of Thomas' bed. It didn't matter whether it was summer or winter, her automatic clock wouldn't let her sleep past first light. As she performed her morning routine, she flicked a gaze into the mirror and paused.

What was she doing? Thomas was a good man born in this valley and, except for a few years, had lived his whole life here. He had roots, just like she did. His great-grandmother was one of the first Norwegian families that homesteaded in Bella Coola after leaving the United States in 1894.

Sonja brushed her tangled hair until her long curls were smooth and silky. Thomas loved her hair. Heck, he loved everything about her. That wasn't her problem. No doubt she loved him too, but could she spend her whole life up here as her parents had? Three years after she graduated from SFU, her dad had a heart attack, and she'd returned to help him and her mother. Then a position came up for a science teacher at McKenzie High, which enabled her to help financially. That was five years ago. Her dad had recovered, and yet, she was still here.

Geography was her specialty, probably encouraged from her fascination with the dramatic continental sheering that created Hunlen Falls, which drained Turner Lake less than two hours east from Bella Coola. One of her professors explained that the Atnarko River at the bottom of Hunlen Falls was North America's original west coast. During the mid-Jurassic age, tectonic interaction between the insular and the intermountain terrains, thrusting up from beneath the ocean floor, had created the coastal mountains. From that presentation onwards, she was hooked. Having returned to the area, she decided to work towards a bachelor's degree in physical geology. Many weekends were consumed with hiking, recording samples and locations, as well as studying previous expeditions in the area.

Sonja jotted a note ending with a happy face, telling Thomas she would see him later, then slipped out to her jeep. She grabbed a scrunchy and pulled her thick hair into a loose ponytail, then rolled the windows down as she headed back home. The air was already warming but still refreshing on her skin as she drove.

Turning on the local radio station, Sonja sang along until a haunting melody, *Breathe* from Faith Hill, triggered thoughts of when she wondered if she'd *ever* find her soulmate. She smiled at the vagaries of fate that led her back to the hometown she'd fled from to travel and see the geological wonders of the world. The only problem was whether to follow her heart and marry Thomas or follow her intellectual dream of exploring new horizons.

Enough. Time to focus on today. Sonja followed her driveway to her back door, where she needed to fill her coolers with ice and one-pound packages of prawn tails. Her dad had taken his traps to his secret spot down one of the fjords and had hauled in over sixty pounds. They'd go quick at the Sunday Market today. Thank God the coolers had wheels at one end. Otherwise, she'd have a hard time lugging them from her house to her jeep.

Her brother, Luke's vehicle, came down the street from their parents' and idled to a stop. He hollered out the window to her, "Sonja! Need a hand? I can take those in my truck if you want."

"That would be great. I promised Mom I'd make lunches for us today. Want to come in and have coffee?"

"Sure, I'll be right in."

Sonja went inside and put a pot of coffee on to brew. She took out a dozen hard-boiled eggs from yesterday and mashed them for deviled-egg sandwiches. Finely chopping celery and green onions, Sonja divided half into the egg mixture and kept the other half for salmon and cream cheese sandwiches. She took the butter and mayonnaise from the fridge, then buttered two loaves of bread. Her family enjoyed their coffee with a muffin on Sundays, preferring a heartier breakfast around ten o'clock in the morning. Then they'd enjoy a late lunch around 2 p.m. before it was time to pack up their stand at the market and head home. Today was their social day of the week, a time to catch up with friends and meet the growing number of tourists who headed to their valley.

"Ready for a sandwich now, Luke?" Sonja stopped wrapping the sandwiches individually in wax paper and offered one to her brother.

"Absolutely." Luke grabbed it and a mug and poured himself a coffee. He gave her a thumbs-up sign as he wolfed down the offering. "Running behind this morning? How come you never have Thomas here overnight? You always go to his place."

"I don't see *you* bringing your girlfriend home to spend the night." Sonja teased.

"That's different. I still don't have my own house. Mom loves Cindy, but I don't want to make it look more serious than it is. Otherwise, Mom will start throwing hints about grandbabies, and I don't want to listen to that. I've noticed she's been giving you hints lately, too."

"I know! How embarrassing. Things are good between Thomas and me, just not sure how far I want it to go. I'm busy teaching and researching for my bachelor's degree. I'm undecided whether I'm ready to settle down and raise a family right now."

"You don't need to have kids right away, just put the guy out of his misery and marry him. "Luke licked his finger and downed the rest of the coffee. "You know you can't find a better catch than him. He'd jump through hoops for you. Besides, you're at his home half the time anyway, so why don't you make it official?"

When no reply was forthcoming, Luke stepped towards his sister, put his hand on her shoulder, and turned her around to face him. "Sonja? Is there a problem you want to talk about?"

"Nope. I know he's great. I couldn't ask for a better man. I'm trying to sort it out." Sonja pulled herself away from him and finished putting water bottles, sodas, and the remaining sandwiches in the cooler. "I'll meet you over at the field in an hour. I still have several things to get ready." Sonja hugged her brother and headed down the hallway.

"Alright, I'll see you later. I'll grab the cooler of prawn tails and bring them to the market for you. Don't forget to bring your bathing suit. Cindy and I are going to Thorsen Creek afterward. You and Thomas are welcome to join us."

"Thanks, Luke. We might just do that." Sonja gave him a finger wave as Luke struggled with the cooler at the back door. As it slammed shut, Sonja retreated to her bedroom and sat on her mattress, breathing a sigh of relief. She felt the subtle pressure from all sides to make a decision. Unfortunately, Sonja was beginning to get itchy feet at the strangest times. Trying to ignore the meaning behind that, she headed for the shower. It would have to be a quick one. Otherwise, she'd end up too late to help Luke erect their tent in a high-traffic location at Lobelco Fairgrounds.

After a long, cold winter, the township couldn't wait for the summer markets to start. Sunday market was a time for getting together and sharing news with the locals, and meeting tourists from all over the world. It wasn't unusual to see a dozen tents erected selling arts, crafts, and homemade food items. Her Uncle Elim's booth usually booked eco-tours for the following week, which provided a much-appreciated additional source of income. He'd be guiding mountain goat and moose hunting expeditions near Bastille Mountain in autumn, where their grandparents had built their first cabin. The log structure was small and rustic but well maintained and served as an excellent base for overnight mountain biking adventures or fall hunting trips.

Sonja stuffed a knapsack with her bathing suit, a change of clothes, and a towel. At this time of year, the weather could transform in a snap. From the mild, breezy morning they had now, it could turn blistering hot or go the other way and produce showers all day. It all depended on the wind's direction. It could be warm from the west or shivering cool from the glacial mountains just east of them. She always tried to be ready for anything.

She wondered if Thomas would join them at the river. He was quite a different man than the one she'd first dated. As an only child, he wasn't always comfortable being in a family group until he began helping his friend Matt construct a retreat. Now, being part of an extended group of people, even if they weren't technically relatives, had made him more open, more friendly, and more approachable.

THOMAS PARKED his car two blocks from the fairgrounds and hitched his backpack on his shoulders. A drumming session ended, followed by light applause. As he came closer, he searched for the white tent topped with the BC flag. Several chairs were situated nearby, where the Hansen family took turns operating their booth and enjoying the activities.

A good turnout today. Probably close to fifteen tents had been erected. Some of the Nuxalk First Nations who attended wore traditional cedar woven hats or blanket and button capes. T-shirts with traditional emblems were a popular sales draw along with handmade treasures. The buzz of chatter and laughter indicated that everyone was in high spirits and ready to be entertained. Thomas perused the crowds and spied Sonja making change for a purchase. He raised his arm and waved, catching her eye.

It felt like his heart doubled in size when she waved back excitedly and motioned for him to join them. She spoke to her brother next to her, then abandoned the table to meet him on the field. "You made it! I was beginning to worry."

"Never worry about me, sweetheart." Thomas put his arms around her and pulled her close, kissing the top of her head. "You look incredibly sexy," he growled in her ear.

"Thanks. I was hoping to find a sexy soulmate here. See any potential candidates?"

"You already have one, so quit looking. Everything you could ever want is right here in front of you." Thomas pulled her in for another kiss and purred softly. "Gotcha."

Sonja swatted his shoulder and winked. "No shortage of self-esteem around here, is there?"

"Nope. So, are you ready for next Wednesday night's market? Anything you need help with?" Thomas asked.

Independent as usual, Sonja shook her head. "No, I'm good. I've got a good selection of both polished and petrified rocks to display. Mom's making mini kransekake rings and her butter cookies to sell. She's also pickled herring for the old-timers. Very few people prepare that anymore."

"Tell her she doesn't need to save any for me. I hate that pickled stuff." Thomas made a face at the thought of it. "Hope there's decent music. It's been a while since we've danced together. I'm going to try and get my friends from Safe Haven to join us and show them how we live it up in the valley." Thomas grinned. "I'm sure it'll be a lot different from what they're used to, but they'll probably find it interesting at least."

"Good thinking. The kids get to meet others at school, but it's harder for the adults. Make sure they come and sit with us when they get here."

"Ok. Speaking of summer events, did you hear the Chamber of Commerce is adding social media to market the rodeo this year? I've heard the town's advertising it from the Nicola Valley right up to Prince George, so they're expecting a big turnout. Party time!" Thomas winked at his beautiful girlfriend. He turned as he heard Eric call his name.

Sonja pulled him back and kissed his cheek. "I'll party

with you anytime." She purred before turning back to her sales table.

"Thomas, I've saved a spot for you." Sonja's dad patted an empty chair beside him.

"Hello, Eric, nice to see you."

"Sonja's almost finished selling the prawns for us. Until she does, come keep me company."

"You've got fresh prawns too?" Thomas asked. "Did you bring your smoked goods today?"

"I did, and it's all gone. I kept a pound of the peppered pink salmon you like. If you need any more, I've got some smoking at home. Just tell my daughter when you want more."

"No, that's enough for this week. So, what's new? Anything interesting?"

"The Chinook run's strong this year. Luke and I are going out again tomorrow morning on low tide. Want to come along?"

"Hmm. I'd love to, but I'm supposed to be putting up fences for the livestock and garden this week. I'll give Matt a call, see if I can postpone a day. He's pretty flexible, so hang on a minute, and I'll make sure."

"We aren't going far. We'll start trolling about halfway down the coast of King Island. And we have a lot of room on our boat. You can ask Matt to come too if you want."

"Are you sure?"

"Of course. Matt's a friend of yours. He's welcome to come."

Thomas called his boss and left a message on his voice-mail outlining the proposal. "He usually gets back to me within the hour, but I'm pretty sure it'll be a go. What time?"

"About five a.m. We'll be home by mid-afternoon."

"Alright, I'll make the lunches and meet you at the boat. Is that ok with you?"

"Sounds good. Coffee will be on." Eric slapped Thomas on his thigh, happy that he was joining him in the morning. "By the way, Thomas. What's taking you so long to make an honest woman out of my daughter?"

"Pardon?" Thomas' face turned crimson as he fumbled for an answer.

"You heard me. How long have you two been going together? Two years?"

"Almost. It'll be two years in October. I'm ready, but when I start hinting about it, she gets nervous and heads home." Embarrassed, Thomas broke his gaze with Eric, searching for Sonja's slim form again, and shrugged. "I'm not sure where I stand with her. Maybe I'm too old."

"Nah. I don't think age's got anything to do with it."

"I don't get it. I've chosen to be alone most of my life, never found anyone I wanted to spend more than a weekend with. Now I want to settle down and have a family." Thomas glanced nervously around them and caught Sonja's gaze staring at him.

She'd kill him if she knew they were talking about her. But, understanding more about her and making her happy was his greatest wish, so he continued. "I need to know if there's a chance for us. It's driving me crazy. Uh-oh, I'm getting the look. Maybe I'll go buy the rest of her prawns."

"Ok, son. We'll talk about this again tomorrow." He shooed Thomas away. "Go, go. Don't keep her waiting. She doesn't have a lot of patience."

∼

A LIGHT FOG hugged the waterline, ensuring a calm surface to navigate. Thomas hefted a cooler bag onboard as Luke untied the vessel from the dock and jumped in.

Thomas grabbed the bumpers and stowed them in the side gunnels. "You weren't waiting for me, were you? It's not even five yet."

"Just having coffee. We came down last night and put ice in the hold and filled the gas tank so we'd be ready to go when you got here. I see Matt didn't come."

"No, he didn't have time to cancel the appointments he had in town today. He said to thank you, and he'd take you up on it another time."

Luke nodded, then ducked inside the cab to speak with his father. When he returned, he lifted the tall Stanley thermos and offered Thomas a mug. "Want a coffee? It's still hot."

"Soon. I just finished one. Is there anything I can do right now?"

"Nope, just sit at the booth. Dad will be cranking it open as soon as the fog lifts. Did you want to jig for cod before we set out the trolling lines?"

"Sure, I'd love to. And I don't have a time frame, so the whole day is free. Whatever you guys want to do is fine with me."

"Dad will be happy about that. At this time of year, he likes to go to Eucott Bay for an hour or two and soak in the hot springs after we've had enough fishing. Have you ever been there?"

"No, didn't even know there was one." Thomas lifted his eyebrow. "Are we allowed to go there?"

"It was probably a sacred site at one time, although now it's a tourist draw. Last time we went around Easter, a helicopter had parked on the flats, so we didn't bother going in."

119

Luke went inside the cab and made himself comfortable at the booth.

Thomas followed him but planted his legs wide apart for balance instead of sitting down. He scrutinized the inlet appearing before him as the fog began to lift. Eric was alternating checking the radar screen and the waters ahead of him, avoiding any drifting logs.

Thomas clasped Eric on the shoulder for a moment. "Thanks for the invite. I haven't been out fishing yet this year. I've been so busy working for Matt, then looking after my own place that I just haven't made time."

"No problem. I've meant to ask you to join us. I figured it was time to get to know you better, especially if you want to be part of the family." When Thomas gulped nervously, Eric chuckled then kept talking, obviously deciding to give him a break. "In about half an hour, we'll be close to Sangster Rock. At this high tide, you'll barely see it breaking the surface, so you'll see the waves first. If we park ourselves east of it, we'll be able to drift close and snag a cod for dinner. I'll keep track of the depth on the radar and move us occasionally while you and Luke do the jigging. Luke will show you where the tackle is. You can use that or get anchovy from the freezer. Whatever you want."

As the wind picked up, the fog cleared, and the steep mountainside fjords of Dean Channel stole Thomas' attention. A light ripple prevented the mirror image on the water, and the low chugging of the diesel engine left a trail behind them. Glancing at his friends' expressions proved that this view never got old for them. Each boating experience had something familiar to appreciate. The eagles high on their perch above a tidal flat searching for their next dinner, or the seals positioned at the mouth of a creek waiting for a returning salmon to enjoy. All of nature in sync with each other.

Thomas turned at the sound of Luke opening a tackle trunk. Inside were layers of trays holding various lures.

"Wow. I didn't think you carried that much."

"When you fish for as long as we have, the collection grows. We take good care of our stuff. Help yourself to your favorite lure."

Thomas prepared two rods for himself, using a purple glow and a sardine Liv Squid. Luke used his lucky rootbeer Liv Squid on both of his lines. The contest details were negotiated, much to Eric's amusement. A ten-spot would reward the largest catch, and whoever caught the smallest legal one would have to gut all the cod before putting them on ice.

LUKE CAUGHT the largest cod at eighteen pounds, but he also hooked the smallest one at seven. Thomas didn't mind handing over the ten-spot when it meant he wouldn't have to clean the four cod brought in. He considered himself a decent fisherman as well as a filet artist, but after watching Luke gut and filet the cod in less than five minutes each, he had to change his opinion of his aptitudes. Not long after, the men finally washed up and were ready to inhale their lunch. Sharing the food with Luke and Eric was entertaining. They loved to tease. He'd need to get ammunition from Sonja so he could dish it right back to them.

Eric finished his sandwich while changing directions for King Island, across from Cascade Inlet. The pinks were starting to return to their roots of origin. Eric watched his sounder, and when he reached the depth he liked, he geared the engines to troll and told the boys to set their rods.

Almost ten o'clock, and they had timed it perfectly. The incoming tide was beginning to run, which would hopefully bring in another school of pinks. Now it was time to keep an eye on their lines for the thrilling tug of a bite. They fished offshore about two hundred feet and settled down patiently. Thomas poured them each a coffee and handed out the rest of the sandwiches to keep their energy up. Once the action started, there'd be no time for eating.

Luke caught the first bite and, like a true fisherman, enjoyed playing it. He set the hook after the line zinged out, then reeled it in, pausing now and then to gauge how tired the salmon was. Luke grinned and let it run when it took off again, then patiently reeled it back in. The pinks here were heavy and strong. It made sense to let them play themselves out.

Luke guided the fish closer to the boat while Thomas eased the net into the water to capture it. A triumphant cheer signaled the landing of a chinook that looked close to thirty pounds. A solid whack knocked the fish out, ending his struggle, and Luke proudly held it up.

Thomas would take a picture of the beauty, but then he saw his rod dip twice before zinging out just as Luke had done. No time to waste now. The bite was on.

"Pull on it, Thomas—lean back and lift your rod high in the air. This chinook's a big one, too." Eric had replaced Luke at the back of the boat and was enjoying the thrill of the sport.

When Thomas finally guided his prize to the boat, Eric expertly netted the fish for him.

"Woo-hoo!" Thomas hefted the salmon up, eyeing the

length of it. "I think I got you beat, Luke. You ready for a rematch?"

"Nah. Let the old man set one up. He usually brings in the biggest catch. We'll see how he does today." Luke made a slow circle and returned the way they came while the guys set their lures again.

When slack tide arrived about four hours later, the men reeled in their rods and tidied the boat. Luke threw a five-gallon pail overboard to fill, then hauled it in and sluiced the deck down, ridding it of the evidence of their day's catch. Eric had caught the largest, probably over forty pounds, while Thomas came in second. Luke snagged two, but both smaller, yet still respectable in the twenty-pound range. A great day.

"Barbecue salmon tonight. I'll give my parents a filet, then bring the rest over to my friends at Safe Haven. They're going to enjoy this." Thomas grinned at the father-son duo. "We'll have ourselves a feast. I'm sure glad I came today. It was amazing. Anytime you want company, don't forget to call. I'll *make* time to join you." Thomas was grinning from ear to ear. Life couldn't be better.

"Finish cleaning the decks, boys, and then we'll head to Eucott Bay. If no one's at the spot, I'll cast an anchor, and we'll take the dinghy to shore. An hour of soaking in the mineral springs helps these old bones." Eric tapped the controls from neutral into low gear, allowing the guys to complete their duties without losing their balance. Once finished, he pushed the throttle down to full gear for the tour to the hot springs.

A half-hour later, Eric slowed his boat, then tapped it into neutral. He checked his sounder for depth then hollered at Luke to heave the anchor. Once the anchor hit bottom, Eric tested the resistance, then satisfied, shut the ignition off. Luke went on the hardtop of the vessel and unhitched the rubber dinghy, sliding it down to Thomas to guide it into the water. Thomas and Eric tied off both ends of the dory and threw the rope ladder over the side for easy access.

"Dad, do you two mind going alone? I've got things to do here while you're gone, and I might just catch forty winks after."

"Sure, do what you want. Thomas can handle the dinghy. We won't be long. Strip to your briefs, Thomas. We don't need more than that."

Thomas followed Eric's lead then went down the short ladder to the dinghy first. He positioned himself to assist Eric, but of course, Thomas refused the younger man's help. Thomas sat and grabbed the oars and began to paddle.

Less than a quarter-mile from shore, it didn't take long for them to reach the enormous slabs of granite that created the natural hot tub for people to enjoy. The steam was rising gently from the surface as Eric threw a weighted rope over to hook the dinghy in place.

"Wow. This hot spring is amazing. Is it very warm?"

"When the tide is low, the water's a little hotter. Right now, the waves break over the walls and cools it down some. It should be almost perfect but watch your step. These slabs have sharp edges."

Thomas balanced precariously between the dinghy and the massive blocks of granite, then threw himself over to stand on the ledge. "Wow, that feels great. How warm do you figure this is?" Thomas grabbed the side of the dinghy for added stability for Eric to exit.

Eric was as sure-footed as ever, barely making a splash before seating himself. "Right now, I'd say around a hundred degrees. At low tide, it'll be a few degrees warmer."

Eric leaned his head against the rock and scanned the sky and trees above them. "Nothing better than this after a day of fishing."

"No kidding. How long have you been coming to this place?"

"Since I was a kid. My father used to visit often. Many mystical moments have happened here. It's a great place to meditate when you have problems on your mind." Eric closed his eyes and breathed deeply.

"Have you brought Sonja here?" Thomas could imagine her in the water with her long blonde hair floating around her. He'd have to bring her sometime soon and skinny dip with her. *Oh, yea*. Thomas' pulse quickened as he imagined sharing this with Sonja.

"Many times. At the end of the last school year, I brought Sonja with a few of her grade ten class who aced their exams. Good incentive."

"That's awesome. Sonja's like you, I guess. She doesn't take nature for granted. That was one of the many qualities I appreciated when we first started dating. She's always thankful for the simplest pleasures and doesn't mind saying it. Most local people usually end up taking it for granted."

"Not surprising when you know her attachment to geology. That girl's always been curious about the history of the land, or anywhere for that matter. It's also what gives her itchy feet."

"Itchy feet? What do you mean?" Ray's eyes narrowed as he tried to figure out if Eric was teasing him.

"She gets travel fever. Anytime she catches a documentary on a location like the Grand Canyon or the mountain peak of Machu Picchu, she gets antsy. She saves a lot of her teacher's salary to see these types of places. The trouble is, she can't make up her mind which one she wants to do first.

And she hasn't found a friend who's willing to travel for months with her. She's not interested in two-week vacations like most people. She wants to *study* these places."

Thomas' eyes widened as Eric continued talking about his daughter. While he knew that Sonja was enamored of the Tweedsmuir Provincial Park and its geology, he didn't realize it was a passion.

"Do you think that's why she's avoiding my marriage proposal?"

"Maybe. We sat around the fire pit last night and had a couple of beers. Sonja talked about you."

"Oh, great. I hope it was good." Thomas frowned, worried what the outcome of their talk had been.

"It was. But you're right. There's a stumbling block. My daughter is nervous about a lifelong commitment to living in Bella Coola. She wants to spread her wings now and then. Travel, see places, live somewhere else for a while."

Thomas watched Eric's gaze, which flitted to the shore, then up to the trees or the sky. Eric avoided looking directly at him. It made Thomas nervous.

What else had Sonja revealed? Thomas felt his face warm up as his heart skipped a beat. Why hasn't she shared this with me? He really should be having this conversation with Sonja, not her dad, but he couldn't wait.

"So, what are you saying? Is she moving? Is she leaving me?"

Thomas watched Eric run his hand over his chin, stalling for time. He finally looked at Thomas directly. "She knows how you feel about staying in this area, and she doesn't want to drag you away. Yet, she wants to be free to go on these adventures too."

Thomas' voice shook in frustration. Spreading his hands in front of him, he replied, "If that's all it is, we can work through that. I wish she would've told me her dreams before. I've been worried that somehow I wasn't enough for her." Thomas blew out a breath he hadn't realized he'd been holding, relieved that travel was the only problem. He let his gaze roam the tranquil setting around him, trying to calm his racing heart.

He glanced back at Eric, noting the compassionate expression on his face. This chat must not have been easy for him either.

"Alright. I get that. Sonja's young. If that's what she wants to do, she should. Once she gets the travel bug out of her system, she might be ready to settle down." His words were clipped, and his voice reflected tension and perhaps a hint of doubt.

"I wouldn't be surprised. My daughter didn't say much, only that she's never felt so safe and loved than when she's with you. It's her adventurous side that's got her confused. Sonja wouldn't want to resent you if she couldn't follow her dreams."

Eric rose from the steaming water and sat on a higher rock to cool. Thomas saw him swallow several times, and his gaze was fixed on a distant object. Something else was bothering him, so Thomas sat patiently, waiting for him to gather his thoughts.

"Not only that, but Sonja thinks we're disappointed that she's not content to live here like we have for three generations. I told her again last night that this is *her* life. Sonja needs to live it passionately, doing the things she loves. As long as our daughter visits and stays in touch with us, we'd give her our blessing."

Blowing out a sigh of parental frustration, Eric continued. "And yet, I'm not sure if that's what she really wants. You're right. Sonja's still young and uncertain about her future. Please don't tell her I mentioned our discussion last night. I felt sorry for you yesterday and had to give you at least an idea why she's been holding out."

"For heaven's sake. We can solve this problem together. I'll work on getting her to tell me more about her hopes and dreams. I would've liked children with Sonja, but I'll support her decision if she decides against it. Whatever makes her happy will make me happy. Nothing else matters."

Eric gestured to the world around them. "This is our passion, your family's and ours. The mountains, the ocean, the land, and the people. But it's not everyone's idea of heaven. Sonja may reach our viewpoint down the road, but she's not there yet. I know it must sound a little crazy, but if you focus on what would mean the most to Sonja, you'll realize that giving her the freedom to travel is the way to go."

"Ok. Thank you for explaining. I've got some serious thinking to do before I talk with your daughter again. But at least I have a direction now."

"Patience, son. She loves you. You two will work it out."

"Thank God, I'm finally at the root of the problem. It explains a lot." Thomas closed his eyes and leaned back, listening to his heart beat faster with new hope. He opened his eyes, scanned the natural beauty around him, and instinctively knew what to do. But first, Thomas must think long and hard to make sure. He didn't want either one of them to have any regrets.

CHAPTER 7 - THE WILSONS

K ari Wilson mixed the last batch of morning-glory muffins and popped them into the oven. When they were cooked and cooled, she'd take them up to the top of the garden where the worker bees were cementing fence posts. Vera was delivering thermoses of coffee and a jug of ice water for them to quench their thirst. Yesterday, they had finished marking the area where the sheep would live in the winter. It would be an excellent job to complete. The final step of stretching the wire around the new posts would seem like child's play compared to the work they'd already done.

Good thing Aaron and Jed were strong and healthy. Every hand helped make the day easier. Ray and Matt had promised the boys free rein on the ATVs after 2 p.m. on weekdays, which served as even more incentive to keep the pace up.

When Kari returned home from the break, she'd make lunches for the boys and Lisa and Chloe to enjoy at their favorite spot in nearby Snootli Creek Park. Kari was pleased with the friendship the two girls shared. Having another girl close to her age made it easier for Lisa to discuss clothes, music, and boys.

Leaving Anna behind in Olympia had been difficult for Matt and the children, but it also affected Kari. She understood her sister's appetite for challenges and her commitment to her coworkers and friends. But truthfully, she wouldn't have stayed behind and let her son and husband leave without her.

Upon arriving in Safe Haven, Lisa had been excited during the first few weeks as everything was new to her. Thank goodness she'd been put in charge of feeding and watering the chicks. It had taken her mind off missing her mom. When the lambs were born, that further encouraged her to be part of the Safe Haven team. Being part of their caretook the sting from her mother's absence.

But Lisa's school days were something else.

Matt had confided in Kari that Lisa was struggling to fit in at school, and he'd caught her crying at night in her room. Kari imagined his awkward attempts to console didn't hit the mark, so she tried to pick up the slack.

The boys enjoyed riding the school bus to SAM Secondary School, but Lisa refused to take the smaller bus to Nusatsum Elementary, where she attended grade seven. This situation meant either Matt, Ray, or Kari had to transport Lisa back and forth. Several times they forgot the afternoon pickup and received a call from a very annoyed young lady. It'd taken a while before they'd organized a schedule that worked for everyone.

Even then, there was often a message from the school to pick up Lisa halfway through the day. Kari wasn't sure if it was cramping from her menstrual cycle approaching or a nervous stomach.

Whatever the cause, she tried her best to console her

young niece and make her feel secure. Carving out girl-time from her community schedule, she encouraged Lisa to bake with her and took her into town at least once a week for an outing. But she could tell from Lisa's moodiness that an aunt was just not the same as a mom.

When Chloe arrived on the scene in late June, Kari was relieved to see the mischief and happiness again in Lisa's eyes. It wasn't just her mother that she missed. It was the loss of the friendships she'd had since grade school.

To Pete and Denyse's relief, the grouchy daughter who'd felt forced to accompany her family to Safe Haven began to shed her anger. Chloe and Lisa had become close friends, always shared tasks, and joined the boys whenever the chance arose.

Kari would be happy when Anna returned, though. She'd seen Jed blushing when Chloe horsed around with his sister and accidentally bumped into him. Although he'd been raised responsibly, at seventeen, he really couldn't help his hormones going into overdrive when a pretty girl was nearby, even if the girl was fifteen. Kari was unsure if Chloe was even aware of Jed's attention.

Luckily, Aaron didn't seem interested in Chloe whatsoever. He was happiest when he was with Jed on the ATVs or with the worker bees building the farm. But she must keep an eye on Jed until Anna returned. Hopefully, she wouldn't need to talk to Matt about his son as well.

"Aunt Kari, I brought you a dozen eggs from the coop. Dad said you'd need them for all the baking you do." Lisa meandered near the counter, eyeing the last batch of muffins cooling on racks. "Do you need help bringing food for the workers? Jed and Aaron moved the picnic table closer to the fence. I think they're getting hungry."

Kari marveled at the change Chloe had made in Lisa's

attitude. Thank God. "Thanks, sweetie. I can always use fresh eggs. Put them in the fridge, please. Those boys are always hungry. It's a full-time job satisfying their appetites. I only have another five minutes to wait before the muffins are cool enough to carry, then you can help me bring them. So, what have you been doing today? I thought you and Chloe were going into town with her mom."

"Not 'til after lunch. And we won't be long, I'm sure. Chloe needs a new bathing suit, and there's not much selection at the Co-op. She'll probably have to order one online, but she says she needs it *now*. We're going swimming with Jed and Aaron later this afternoon, and Chloe said she was embarrassed the last time she wore her suit."

"I have a stretchy halter top that's good for swimming but is now too small for me. I loved it too much to throw it away. A woman can always hope she'll get back to her younger figure, but the reality is I won't. Tell Chloe she can have it if she strikes out shopping and wants to use my halter top with her shorts for swimming."

"Ok. Mike finished mucking out the barn and feeding the pigs while we fed our chicks, so we'll be free for the rest of the afternoon. Those chicks have doubled in size and have most of their feathers now. I guess they'll be going into the coop soon. I hope we get more like Thomas promised." Lisa plopped onto the kitchen stool, watching her aunt. "He wants to have lots of roasting chickens in the freezer for the winter. I'm glad I don't have to be around when they get butchered. I couldn't handle that."

Lisa dipped her hand into the bag of raisins near her and munched as she switched subjects. "Did I tell you I went up to the main lodge and talked to Mom last night on Facebook Messenger?"

"That's good. How's my sis doing?" Kari washed the

utensils she'd used while baking. Some days it was hard to live without a dishwasher. It seemed her hands were always in soapy water and were showing it—a small price to pay to avoid an electrical burnout, she supposed. Every bit helped. Kari was so much more aware of power usage since they'd come to Safe Haven. It had been a hard habit to grow into, making sure power usage was kept at a minimum.

"I thought she'd lost weight, but she says she hasn't. She seemed happy. She told her boss that she'd be leaving by the end of July. So, we finally have a date when she'll join us. That was pretty exciting news."

"I'll bet. We all miss your mom. I'm glad everything turned out better than we thought it might at the hospital. At least she'll be here for part of the summer. Your dad and Jed must be thrilled as well."

"Oh, yea. I was online with Mom first, and then Dad took over. He came home with the biggest smile on his face, praising the Lord for answering his prayers. He was always worried about her, but I knew she'd be ok."

"How did you know that? Are you clairvoyant?" Kari teased.

"What's that?"

"It means you're psychic. You can see the future." The oven timer rang, and Kari shut the oven off, removing a tray of muffins to the counter to cool. "Some people claim to have ESP, and occasionally I wonder if your mom and I don't share that. You know the feeling when someone needs help or is anxious, and you phone them and find out something important was going on? And you say, *I knew it. I had a feeling*. That's usually what people mean when they say they have ESP."

"Yea. But it could just be that they know the other person so well, they can guess what they'll do."

"That's more probable than ESP. Still, I've heard strange stories. It makes me wonder. I'm just thankful I'll have my sister with us soon."

"So am I. You've taught me a lot about cooking, Aunty, but I'll be glad not to do that job so often. And I think Dad and Jed are going to puke if I make one more spaghetti sauce."

Kari burst into laughter. "True enough. You can only eat pasta for so long before you can't stand the sight of it. Listen, I've taken out two chickens to roast tonight. Do you want to have dinner here?"

"You bet I do. I'll tell Dad. What time do we need to be home from swimming?"

"Make it six. Then we'll eat around 6:30. That should leave you plenty of time, right?"

"I guess so. Maybe you should ask Aaron and Jed. Chloe and I are only along for the ride. I have no clue how long it takes to get anywhere. I just follow the back of Aaron's head and then Chloe and Jed's when they get close."

"Ok. Grab the basket of muffins on the counter. Vera should be heading up there now with the coffee. Tell everyone I'll be there very soon."

WALKING up the hill towards the barn, Kari passed Pete, Mark, and Gwen working in the garden. "The vegetables are flourishing in this beautiful weather. Are those beans sprouting?" Kari pointed to a tall triangular structure with green foliage creeping up.

"Yes, they're beginning to flower. This heat's been excellent for the vegetables. We're even spacing our carrots and beets now. Everything's growing very well." Gwen stood straight and arched her back. "Pete's in charge of the cukes and tomatoes, and he says they're the size of a quarter right now, so that's welcome news considering we had to plant them twice."

"Damn deer. Cute, but they can level a garden pretty quick. Why don't you take a break? Coffee and muffins are heading to the fence line. Come join us."

"You don't have to tell me twice." Mark leaned his hoe against the wheelbarrow and removed his gloves.

Gwen and Pete joined him as they followed Kari to the picnic table.

"Looking good, fellas. How many more posts to cement?" Pete asked.

"About twenty. Tomorrow we'll backfill the holes. By Thursday, we'll start stretching the wire and pounding the staples in. Thank God, we'll finish before the August heat hits us." Thomas removed his hat and gloves, then wiped his brow. "Thanks, Kari, for the muffins. It seems like breakfast was a long time ago." Thomas walked over to the outdoor faucet they had run to the fence line and washed quickly.

Ray and the boys followed suit, then returned to the picnic table and helped themselves to the muffins and coffee. "Hey, fellas. We've done really well with fence posting both the garden and the livestock area. I think we should think about changing the hours we work here. It's getting hotter all the time. What do you think about starting between six and seven o'clock, then calling it quits early in the afternoon until it cools off in September? On hot days we should be out of the sun by two max. That's what we used to do in construction during the summer. Nobody benefits if we get heatstroke."

"I'm an early bird, Ray," Matt commented between sips of coffee. "So, I don't have a problem with that. I'd prefer to work in the cool morning anytime. I'm glad you brought the subject up. I'll post a notice on the board about the new hours, so everyone's aware."

Kari looked at each of them, realizing they were all on board, except for Jed and Aaron, of course. She'd let them know they didn't have to come until 8 a.m. They were just boys, after all, and entitled to enjoy their summer too.

Aaron had followed Jed's lead, stripped off his shirt, and splashed water on himself before joining the crew. Kari noticed this summer's work had developed muscles across their shoulders and arms. Anna was going to be surprised to see how much they had both grown.

Jed and Aaron had definitely left the gawky teenage years behind them. Even Mike had more stamina than he had when he first arrived.

When Ray appeared next to her, she gave him a mug of water. She knew he wouldn't eat right away, at least not until he had cooled down.

As usual, Ray's skin had already tanned to a golden brown. With pride, she noted he was the healthiest of the lot of them. In top physical shape from years of physical labor, he had the strength of two men. She wiped away a trickle of sweat that dripped from his hairline, down his temple. She smiled as she caught his gaze.

"I've invited Matt and the kids for roast chicken tonight. Lisa was hinting for an invite, so I thought I'd give them a break."

"Too bad. I had an idea to take you swimming after supper." He leaned close to her ear and whispered. "Skinny dipping would've been fun."

Kari giggled as she stroked her husband's arm discreetly. "No one will last long after dinner. If I know the kids, they'll want to make a fire and sit around for the evening. And Matt looks beat. Are we taking the truck or an ATV?"

"ATV. We can find more private spots with that. Bring a bottle of wine and pack a pair of travel mugs in my backpack, alright?"

"You bet. Can't wait." Kari gave him a wink and returned to hand out more refreshments.

ALL THROUGH DINNER AND CLEAN-UP, Ray couldn't keep his eyes off his wife. She positively glowed with vitality as she teased and fed the crew. Lisa helped with clearing the table and never even thought twice about picking up the dish towel to dry dishes. All of the kids had come a long way since they moved here four months ago.

Adjusting to school life was the hardest, but the boys had it easier than Lisa. Jed and Aaron had each other and were quickly involved in extracurricular sports, which triggered new friendships easily. Lisa was always shy, so it hadn't been as easy for her. Now she seemed back to her usual self since Chloe arrived, which made both families feel good.

Kari had been correct in assuming the house would be deserted soon after dinner. With everyone having their own agenda, she and Ray were ready to explore the area by themselves. At 7:00, the sun hadn't even begun to set behind the high mountains surrounding them. This far north, they would have dusk until at least ten o'clock at night. Plenty of time to enjoy being alone together.

Ray grabbed two towels and the backpack, smiling as he anticipated the evening ahead. Telling their kids they were heading towards Snootli Creek, they left Safe Haven and headed southwest.

Matt had bought and mounted GPS monitors on each of the four ATVs as a precaution if anyone became disoriented and couldn't find their way home. Better safe than sorry. And heading out so late, tonight might be one of those times they'd finish the trip in the dark.

Ray thought he knew the area well enough to manage getting home without help, but he felt better knowing it was available if needed.

Checking over the ATV before leaving, he noted the boys had remembered to fill the tank up for the next person and that it had been tidied and wiped down. Nothing worse than having to do those things when you are in a hurry to get somewhere. He pulled his helmet on, then started the engine and put it into first gear to pick up his wife.

They were both wearing long jeans to avoid the mosquitos and no-see-ums that would be active at nightfall. As Kari approached the machine, he threw her a helmet and watched her giggle as she dropped her knapsack to catch it.

"Smart ass." She pulled the chin straps tight, then shrugged the backpack on her shoulders and sat behind him, holding him close. "Ok, big boy—let's go!"

That's all the encouragement Ray needed. He took the quickest route into the trees to avoid creating a dust field behind them. After a while, he slowed down and pointed out areas Kari hadn't seen before. They climbed to the hilltop where their families had first surveyed their property and learned of their future.

"Let's stop here for a bit." Ray parked the machine near the firepit and removed his helmet, with Kari following suit.

"Wow. You can barely see the buildings now. All the

leaves have blocked them out. It looks a lot different than last winter." Kari grabbed the binoculars from her knapsack. "I see the corner of the main lodge, the barn, some animals, and the lean-to shelters further down the property, but I can't see our homes through the foliage. It's so beautiful from up here, a perfect snapshot for farming life."

Ray snuck up behind her and wrapped his arms around her middle, snuggling her neck. Their new life was different from the city, exciting and challenging in its own way. He hoped she was glad they had come. Even if it turned out they had been over-cautious, it was better than living in fear. "Are you still ok with the move, sweetheart?"

"Yes. It'll be even better when Anna's here with us. Don't get me wrong, though. I'm still not sure I'm ready to spend the rest of my life in Safe Haven, but it's a great change. I'm not going to worry about our future. I plan on concentrating on today, this week, this year. I've never been able to look down the road and feel comfortable. Too many people pin their hopes of where they'll be in twenty years, then are disappointed."

"That's what I've always admired about you. Living in the moment and enjoying it. We'll deal with the future when it arrives."

"I wish Matt felt the same. He's so preoccupied trying to prepare that he forgets to enjoy time with his family *now*. It's been hard on their kids. I'm glad Anna will join us soon. Maybe she can tone him down."

"Maybe. Time to hop back on our ATV if you want a swim." This time Ray handed Kari her helmet, then replaced his and started the ATV. They left the hilltop in the opposite direction, making their way descending through the brush carefully.

When Kari tapped his shoulder, he stopped and shut off the motor.

"Look at the size of that cedar!" Kari jumped off and ran to it, stretching out her arms to estimate its circumference. "It's huge. Come hold my hand and see if we can circle it."

Ray stepped carefully around the giant ferns on the forest floor as he joined Kari. "I'd say we're over halfway around, so the circumference must be close to fifteen feet. These are actually two trees that have grown together at the base. The diameter of each must be nearly four feet, making them around a hundred years old."

"Amazing." Kari scoured the forest floor then bent to inspect a clump of delicate white trillium blossoms.

Ray knew by her darting gazes that she wished she'd brought her camera. The evening light filtered through the evergreens, casting shadows around them, creating intriguing discoveries of mushrooms and berries.

"We'll come again, Kari. You can get your fill of photography another day. Watch your step coming back this way. It's muddy."

Kari straightened and assessed her situation. She'd wandered a hundred feet away from the ATV in an upward direction. His wife had paid no attention to the squishy ground and mossy areas, but now she'd have to be careful picking her footsteps back. She put her hands out to balance herself and began the descent. Suddenly, her foot slipped forward in the mud, and she lost her balance. With a yelp, she put her hands down to help break her fall.

Ray chuckled as he saw his independent wife lose her battle with the muddy decline. He had thought of offering his assistance, but he knew from experience that she wouldn't want it.

He watched as her head snapped up and caught his

gaze, her eyes narrowing in a warning. *Not a word*, it conveyed. She massaged her left wrist for a few seconds, then picked herself up and made her way to him, limping slightly.

"It's easy to get carried away and go farther than you should. You want a towel for your hands?"

"No." Kari wiped her hands on her jeans. "We should be close to the river. I'll clean up there."

"Are you ok? Anything hurt?" Ray hopped onto the ATV and slipped his helmet on again.

"Not really. A little sprain, but nothing I can't handle. Let's go." Joining her husband, she hung onto him as they followed the Snootli Creek trail past the Beaver Pond and down to the riverside.

The exposed round river rocks would make it hard for Kari to walk, so he brought his machine right to the water's edge. Ray cleared a small space in the sun to place their blanket, then helped Kari slip out of her jeans. He took them, and her runners rinsed them in the creek and then laid them upside down to drain and dry for the trip home.

"How cold's the creek?" Kari asked as she prepared to join him.

"It's chilly. The mountains still have a snow pack. I think it will be a quick dip for me."

"Chicken." Kari drew her T-shirt over her head and finished undressing.

Ray watched his wife strip as he quickly shucked his own clothes, tossing them on the rocks. He helped her up and gave her his arm to lean on. "No sense in straining that ankle. You want me to pick you up?"

"I can manage, although come to think of it, it might be a good idea." She wrapped her arms around his neck as he picked her up.

Ray felt a shiver run through his wife as she pressed her naked body close to him. He felt her nipples harden as they brushed against his chest hair. Her body temperature was much cooler than his, and Ray saw goosebumps forming on her. He could hardly wait to heat that satiny skin to a flush.

He picked his way carefully to the shoreline and into the darker and deeper part of the creek, hissing his shock at the icy, fast-flowing water. When Ray reached his thighs, he let her down, laughing at her expression.

"Holy crap!" Kari washed her hands quickly, then, before losing her courage, took a shallow dive. She trod water for a moment. "C'mon in, the water's beautiful."

"Like hell it is...you're just trying to lure me." Ray started to turn to shore before her taunting laughter dared him to return. He took a deep breath, leaped, and immersed himself in the water between them.

The satisfied look on his wife's face made the plunge worthwhile. He pulled her tightly into his arms and kissed her chilly, wet lips. He felt the light breath of urgency on his neck and picked her up quickly. "Enough of that. We need to warm ourselves up. Got any ideas?"

Ray sloshed his way back to shore, depositing Kari on the blanket. He sprinted to his backpack on the ATV and withdrew the towels, returning to wrap one around her. He rubbed her briskly to take the chilly edge off.

Towel drying his hair and wiping himself down, he sat beside her and grinned. "You'd think we were teenagers. I'll say something for cold water, though. I was feeling tired after the job we did today, but not anymore. My energy's back, and I know exactly how to use it." Ray's eyebrows danced before he continued. "Although may have to coax my friend back from that icy dip." Ray scooted over to his wife and pulled her close before lowering his mouth to taste those tempting lips.

Her immediate response thrilled him as his body temperature quickly returned to normal.

Kari laid back against the blanket and drew him next to her. He saw her eyes dancing mischievously as her hands traced his muscles from his chest downward. Ray gave her a head start before he began his journey down the curves of the woman he'd married almost twenty years ago. Moving here had brought them even closer together, and Ray thanked God for the day they found each other. The sound of the creek rushing over river rocks became nature's music as they found pleasure in making the other happy.

Suddenly, Ray stopped. He put a finger to his lips for her to be quiet as he searched the source of the disturbance. Kari stilled immediately, slowly becoming aware of the noise her husband had probably heard. There was movement in the brush only a hundred feet away. His gaze caught Kari's as he slowly got to his knees.

"Bear. Move slowly and put your shoes on." Ray fumbled in his jeans pocket and got the keys out. Just as a large black bear lumbered across the rocks, he started the ATV and revved its motor.

The bear stopped in his tracks and lifted his nose in the air, poised to react.

Kari threw on her T-shirt and panties, then jumped on the back of the ATV. The roar of the engine revving seemed to have startled the bear. It turned and retreated into the bush.

Ray felt Kari's arms tighten around his waist while her knees clamped against his hips. He continued to gun the throttle for another minute before shutting off the engine.

"I think he's gone now. He probably came down to the

creek for a twilight feeding. You did good, but I think we'd better grab our stuff and get the hell out of here."

"I'm more than ready to head out. We don't have to go back through the trails, do we?"

"No, we'll cross downstream at the bridge, then follow the highway. We'll be home within a half-hour that way."

"Thank God. Nature's beautiful, but—"

"I know. I'll ask Thomas for advice on safer places to visit." Ray rolled up the wet clothes in the towel, then folded the blanket and strapped them to the rear of the ATV, then returned to help his wife.

She hung on his arm while she favored her left ankle. They'd enjoy the wine back home in front of a fire, warm and safe.

CHAPTER 8 - COMING TOGETHER

Anna knew Matt was disappointed that she hadn't yet arrived, but not everything in life could be controlled. She was glad that he was supportive of her situation, even though it created more problems for him.

After Anna helped her friend through a bout of Legionnaire's disease, she had kept an eye on Gina's return to health. Slowly but surely, Gina regained her strength and could fully participate in home duties and resume quality time with her family.

Anna had told Matt that Gina began working two days a week last month at the hospital, which had perked her spirits up considerably. Unfortunately, a week ago, a heart attack had taken the life of her husband, Ron. It was an unexpected blow for the family. An aortic aneurism had burst with absolutely no warning, throwing the family into chaos.

Anna had already packed the things she was taking to Bella Coola. She'd had her farewell party from the hospital and said goodbyes to her close friends. Anna gave the food in her downstairs suite to the Lee family upstairs.

Everything was clean, ready for the new tenant from Lisa's school. Ted was a custodian newly arrived from Seattle and needed furnished accommodations nearby. In his fifties, his gentle manner had won Anna over, and she signed a one-year lease with him. A dependable handyman was a good solution for their rental home.

When Gina's daughter, Jan, called Anna with the news of her father's passing, Anna was caught in a difficult situation. Everything was packed, and she was due to leave her home on Thursday to drive to Port Hardy and catch the ferry.

She called Matt and discussed her dilemma. Having already taken more time than she initially thought was necessary for her job, she hated to ask for more. Thankfully, it was Matt who suggested she remain behind for another few weeks to ensure Gina could adapt to the tragedy.

After all, it was summertime, and what was a couple more weeks?

Grateful for Anna's assistance, Gina insisted that Anna save the cost of renting a hotel room. Anna could bring her things to Gina's place and use the spare bedroom while sorting the mess Gina's life had become.

Jan was appreciative of Anna's help. She had a hard enough time looking after her two young children and coming to terms with losing her father. With Anna supporting Gina, it would allow Jan to become the pillar of strength she'd need to be for her mom.

AND SO, the first few weeks of August continued without Anna in Safe Haven. Matt tried to set an example of understanding and compassion so Anna's sister and her children could follow in his footsteps. He was beginning to wonder if his wife would ever get there and be the mother she used to be.

It seemed to be one thing after another, and in his darkest moment, he questioned Anna's priorities. Then as he contemplated in prayer every night, he was reminded of their love and her compassion. He realized that patiently waiting for his wife was the least he could do.

After the Sunday service ran by Denyse, Matt held an impromptu meeting. He discussed the need for all-hands-on-deck this coming week. Mid-August meant it was time to harvest the earliest crops and begin the preservation process.

Vera organized a schedule, and volunteers signed up for extra hours. Chloe and Lisa would pick the pea pods, shell them, then bring them to the central lodge kitchen, where Vera would blanch them for two minutes before draining and dumping them in a tub of ice water. Gwen would scoop them out and drain them in colanders when the vegetables were chilled before laying them on cookie trays and flash freezing them. Later, they would vacuum pack them into two-pound packages and freeze them. After chopping green beans and carrots, the ladies would repeat the process.

It made sense for everyone to pitch in and create an assembly line to preserve their garden goods as quickly and efficiently as possible. The good-natured ambiance warmed Matt's heart when he'd enter the lodge where music blared, and people laughed while working for their common good.

Meanwhile, Ray and Thomas were building storage racks providing air circulation that they'd use in the basement of the utility garage. The potatoes would be cured there before boxing with shredded paper. This method would ensure quality potatoes for most of the winter. Pete and Vera were busy hanging garlic and onions to dry outdoors before boxing into cold storage.

After checking Pete's tomatoes, Ben declared many of them could be picked and stored there as well. The best time to pick them was when there was still green on the tomato, and the colors were transitioning to yellow and a hint of pink. This method ensured the best nutrient value and encouraged the tomato plant to continue to produce. Checking the trays every few days allowed Pete and Denyse to can them whole, chopped, or make them into relishes and salsas at a more leisurely schedule.

Kari loved freezing fruit and making jams to enjoy throughout the year. Thomas' parents had apple, plum, and pear trees. The fruit trees recently planted on their land wouldn't be yielding very much for at least two years, so sharing the preserves with the Kerrs was a win-win situation. She volunteered to organize work bees to produce the frozen, dried, and canned fruit they would enjoy in all seasons.

Jed and Aaron offered to pick blackberries when they got tired of prepping fish or chopping wood. Thomas and Mark had joined forces to process fish outdoors in pressure cookers or by smoking and freezing.

Everyone had their specialty. A sense of belonging grew stronger as the community members pooled their energies into providing a food supply. Whenever anyone had spare time from their assigned duties, it became common for them to help out in another area. It made Matt proud to see the fellowship within the retreat. It became a habit for him to visit each worksite near the end of the day, complement his team, and share a prayer of thanks.

As Matt finished his bank reconciliation, he thought about his extended family, who were growing so close together. He could see the love and respect building between each family. In September, Matt would need to deal with the money aspect of their community. He'd asked everyone to just look after their utility bills until the fall when he'd be able to have a good idea of his operating costs by then. He'd invested almost everything he had into this place, but he had to be realistic.

He prayed for guidance to find the right way to manage this haven equitably. Matt had faith that the answer would become apparent soon.

He glanced at his watch and jumped to his feet. The ferry from Port Hardy would dock within the hour. No one knew of Anna's arrival today.

Matt hoped to meet his wife in Campbell River for a few days, but too much was happening here. He still wanted time to themselves before sharing her with Lisa, Jed, and the rest of the family. Matt grabbed his keys and left the compound, heading for the grocery store to buy a bouquet of red roses or carnations, depending on the availability. He planned to take her to dinner at the Eagle Lodge, known for its fresh seafood and succulent steaks. Add a good bottle of wine, and it should take the edge off the long trip to her new home.

Matt's pulse raced as he examined his image in the mirror before heading out the door. He felt as nervous as a young suitor as he checked the pressed khaki pants and an open-necked blue polo shirt. After lunch, he had freshened up and pulled out Anna's favorite men's cologne. He smacked his cheeks like he used to do when they went somewhere special, which seemed like eons ago. He felt as giddy and horny as a teenager.

$\sim$

"MATT, oh my Lord, look at you!" Anna hurried to him, dropping her suitcase and purse by her side and wrapping her arms around him. She felt his smooth, close-shaven face and inhaled the scent of Obsession. Anna closed her eyes as a wave of heat surged through her. Drawing back, she looked into his eyes again, noting the moisture in them.

"Anna. Thank God. I couldn't have waited much longer. Let me look at you." Matt scanned her from top to bottom. "Perfect. Just perfect. As always. I'm so excited that I could almost yell my thanks to heaven." Matt drew her to him again, holding her tight and rocking from side to side. "Where's your things, honey? You must have more than this one suitcase."

"Yes, everything is tagged and labeled. The staff is going to put my things in the terminal for us to pick up. They told me to give them an hour to get it there, so we've time to walk and talk. I left my SUV with a storage outfit in Port Hardy. This way, we won't need to spend the money bringing our vehicles back and forth."

"That was a great idea. I've made dinner reservations for us at the Eagle Lodge. No one knows you're coming today. I've told Ray I had business in town tonight. I'll apologize when I get home, but I need to spend time alone with you. Once you get to Safe Haven, you know we won't have five minutes to ourselves for a few days."

"Good idea." Anna surveyed the changes in her husband in the last six months.

He seemed a little trimmer, a little more muscular around his upper torso. And a sprinkling of grey had started around his temples. This spring and summer had been a difficult culmination of years of planning. He earned every one of those silver threads.

"Tell me about the kids. How are they *really* doing?

When I ask you on Zoom, I can tell that they're nearby, so I don't know if I'm getting the full story. And when I talk to them, they still seem excited about the place and always busy doing something. I never hear about any problems, so it's made me wonder."

"They're doing well, even Lisa. Ever since Chloe came up, the girls have been enjoying each other's company. Lisa will be heading up to SAM Secondary in September along with Chloe and the boys. That should make life easier for her than last year. She's been babysitting quite a lot, with Kari's supervision, of course. I'll let her tell you more. Right now, I want to know how *you're* feeling. It must've been hard leaving Gina when she's so vulnerable after Ron's death." Matt led her to the vehicle and handed her the bouquet of red carnations and baby's breath he'd just purchased.

"You remembered the color of my bridal bouquet! Thank you, sweetheart." Anna drew in the scent of her bouquet, then leaned forward and pulled him over for a long, tantalizing kiss. They broke apart, smiling in anticipation of more to come later.

They drove the short distance to the Eagle Lodge. Once seated, Matt ordered a bottle of Grey Monk Pinot that he knew Anna favored for special occasions. He held her hand across the table, and she felt herself glow with happiness as she scanned the scenery outside the picture window. The snow-tipped, rugged mountains surrounding them sparkled in the afternoon sun. The last time Anna was here was in the winter when they couldn't see the summits.

"It's beautiful here, honey, and now that you're home, life will be so much better. I was worried for a while that you'd change your mind." Matt kissed her fingers. "I'd almost forgotten how beautiful you are. Have I told you how happy I am that you're home?"

151

"Only a couple of times." Anna smiled. "I've missed you and the kids so much that it was easier to work long hours than to wonder how you were managing. No regrets, though. I did an important job. Now our hospital is prepared to handle anything that comes."

"Good. Now that it's finished, I hope you'll be happy here. I don't regret the move I made to get this place ready, either. Yet, I wish I would've been brave enough to tell you about it, to include you in all the decisions. That won't happen again, I promise."

"I think we both learned something about secrets. I'll keep in touch with my friends while we're here, especially Gina. However, even she can't make up for not having you and the kids beside me. Lisa and Jed will be surprised when I arrive tonight."

"Let's pick up pizzas to bring home, so we don't have to fuss with dinner. Everyone will be too excited about seeing you to bother with making a proper meal anyway."

"Good idea." Anna sipped her wine again, and as she watched her husband, she slowly ran her tongue around her upper lip.

She saw his eyes light up at her invitation.

"Can't wait to sit by the fireplace tonight. Eventually, the kids will go to bed, and I intend to spend the rest of the night making you ecstatic that you're here with me. Unless you have other plans?" Matt raised his eyebrow, daring her to refuse.

"I've been dreaming about this for a long while. Nothing else is more important." Anna squeezed her husband's hand tightly and raised her glass. "To us and our new life."

"To us and a new beginning." Matt clinked glasses, then opened the menu to order.

ANNA HUMMED as she put on a fresh pot of coffee, then collapsed on the kitchen chair. What a whirlwind the last day had been. So many hugs and kisses and half-told stories. Her lonely heart filled with the love she received.

And much later, Matt showed her exactly how much he missed her. She'd never felt so complete and whole. Anna blushed as she relived the ecstasy they shared last night. Anna returned the attention, patiently teasing him into a repeat performance. It was no surprise that Anna slept in this morning until almost ten o'clock. She never even heard Matt and the kids moving around or leaving the house.

This morning she was unpacking the boxes of treasured items she couldn't bear to leave in storage, then began to put her clothes away. She looked in the cupboards and realized she'd need to reorganize them, but on the whole, they had done a great job arranging her home. She heard a quick knock at the back door, then it opened. Kari walked in with a coffee mug in her hand.

"Morning, sweetie. You don't know how much I missed you, Anna. I hope it's ok that I just popped over. I'm afraid I might be a pest for a while."

"Don't be silly." Anna got up and hugged her sister. "Anytime you want to come over, just make yourself at home. Coffee's almost ready. Need more?"

"Sure." Kari sat and looked around at the littered counters and tables filled with things that needed to find a home. "Do you need help with this? Or do you want to do it yourself?"

"I'm not in a hurry. I'll manage. I'd rather hear about the kids. Tell me all about them. It's amazing the difference in both Aaron and Jed. The muscles! They're young men now."

"The boys are great. They've taken on a lot of responsibilities around here, helping the men with the big projects. They've definitely matured in their attitude about things too."

"Matt said he was proud of them. And Lisa and Chloe have been quite helpful too. I hear Lisa's even babysitting Tyler and Troy when their parents go out on a day trip in the mountains."

"Yes, she's good with them, plays with them, and is very patient, so she makes all the money. Chloe refuses to babysit. She'd rather work with the animals or help her parents now and then with the garden."

"So, what else are they up to? They can't be working all summer around here."

"Matt has organized it so they all have jobs to do in the morning starting around nine o'clock, then they're free to make their own decisions for the afternoon. The boys help the guys with the big projects like fencing or chopping wood, but otherwise, they take off on the ATVs and explore. Often, they take the girls swimming at the river or one of the creeks around here."

"Good. Teenagers need to have fun. Anything else I should know?"

"Not really. We just finished a few crazy weeks preserving our vegetable garden. Even the kids were helping to chop and package them. Next came how to filet and can salmon, and Sonja spent a weekend giving recipes and tips on smoking salmon with different brines. We've all learned a lot in just one summer, that's for sure."

"I hope Lisa will be more agreeable with school this year. Having Chloe in the same school should make a difference. It'll be easier on us having all the kids at SAM High."

"Definitely. It should cut down on the amount of driving

back and forth for school. Maybe they'll get their act together as a pack and be on time for the bus. Anyway, you'll be here to help me keep them organized with the school activities. An extra hand goes a long way."

"I'm sure it's going to make your life easier now. I can't thank you enough for stepping in and helping Matt with the kids."

"You're welcome. I enjoyed helping Jed and Lisa. I think you're going to be pleasantly surprised when you meet the rest of the crew here. We've managed to be friendly and helpful without being in each other's back pocket. Gwen reminds me a little of Gina. Speaking of Gina, how's she handling things?"

Anna got up to pour them each a refill of coffee as she thought of her answer. "As well as can be expected, I guess. Ron was only sixty-one years old." She shook her head as she relived the jolt that rocked Gina's world. "I've promised to Zoom with her at least once a week. I've always been able to read her like a book, so I'm sure I'll be able to help her get through this, even if it's long-distance."

"Jan and the grandkids will help, I'm sure."

"They will. Last week, I helped Gina empty the closets of Ron's clothes. I brought them to the Salvation Army, who will put it to good use." Anna tapped her forefinger on her cup as she remembered the crisis. "That was a tough day— even harder than the day of the funeral service. She kept a stiff upper lip throughout the memorial for her family and friends, but she was a mess the day we tackled the closets. She'd go from tears to shock as she folded his clothes into the boxes. It took the whole day to relate memories of him wearing them. There were a few items she just couldn't part with. It was so sad." Anna sniffled as she remembered the day and hunted for a tissue.

"You're her best friend, so of course you hurt for Gina. I'm glad you stayed longer to be with her. It wouldn't have been easy to be up here, knowing what she had to go through without you."

"I know. Gina didn't have a sister, so I'm glad I could help. I know she'd be there for me too if I had problems."

"We don't listen to the American news very much up here, just bits and pieces. Was Matt right? Is it worse?"

"It's not any better, that's for sure. There's still a lot of hostility over the lack of housing and shortages. It depends on which side of the fence you're on. Some are complacent and figure it will all work out one day, but those are ones established with their own homes. The people who were forced to move north are becoming angrier and louder. Low-cost housing projects are popping up here and there, but not fast enough to meet the need. I've seen one constructed in Tutweiller, and I'm afraid it's going to turn into a slum area very quickly. Long narrow container units were refurbished into family units of a thousand square feet, then stacked four stories high. Then, they hide the structure with siding. It's better than nothing, but not by much."

"Yikes, that's scary."

"It is. There have been articles in the paper that more medical clinics will be set up in malls around the state to ease emergency visits to the hospital. Online consultations with nurse practitioners are also being encouraged to lower wait times and costs. And the governor is advertising throughout the states to new medical graduates to relocate there in return for a tax break."

"It sounds like they're making an effort. What about the schools?" Kari's eyebrows furled to the center, and Anna knew her sister was thinking of the district where she was employed. The school system was over-stressed when Kari left there six months ago.

"There are discussions of how to address that. The quickest solution is to add more portables to schools that have room for them. I've also heard talk of having more online programs for students to study at home, then they'd come in one or two days a week for projects or testing. I don't think that's a good option, but maybe short-term, that's all they'll be able to do."

"Groceries and gas? Any changes there?"

"No. Prices are rising steadily. Remember when we used to shop after work or in the evenings? Forget it. By then, there's very little to choose from unless you're buying tinned goods. You have to be quick and shop early to keep your cupboards stocked." Anna leaned forward, her left eyebrow raised. "Do you know what the growing industry is in Washington State? Food banks. Can you believe it? On the other hand, I see more communities pulling together to help each other. It's not an easy place to breathe, you know?"

"It's hard to breathe deeply when you're scared." Kari sighed. "Part of me feels guilty for abandoning my country. The other part is extremely thankful to be out of there. I only hope the situation doesn't get worse."

"Me too. I just pray that Washington doesn't start having their natural catastrophes like Matt believes are coming. Let's hope those times are decades away. Let's get rid of one problem before dealing with another." Anna stood up and put her cup in the sink. "That's enough caffeine for me. Time to get back to work. What are you doing next?"

"I'll go see who needs help with what. The boys picked a couple of gallon pails of blackberries yesterday, so I might make jam this afternoon." Kari gave her another hug. "Welcome home, sis. You'll find me in the main lodge if you need me."

ANNA STORED the last suitcase away when she heard the backdoor slam and footsteps thump down the hallway. She turned the corner in time to see Lisa slam the door to her bedroom.

"Lisa? What's going on?" Anna knocked lightly on her daughter's door. She could hear angry mumbling and paper ripping. She opened the door carefully. "Wow. Who pissed you off?"

Posters had been ripped from the wall, then shredded onto her bed and the floor. Lisa turned and glared at her mom, then pushed her aside and sprinted from her room.

Anna's shock temporarily paralyzed her. Her daughter had never gone off the deep end before, acting frantic like that. What the heck? Anna heard the door slam again and raced outside to the porch, watching her daughter sprint toward the barn.

"Lisa? Lisa!" Anna knew her daughter could hear her, yet Lisa refused to answer.

What was that all about? Remembering arguments with her sister at that age, she gave Lisa a minute to cool off before approaching. Hot-tempered discussions wouldn't end positively. Anna returned to Lisa's bedroom in search of clues. As she picked up the pieces, she realized they were pictures of Lisa and Chloe having fun this summer. Uh-oh. Something between them must have upset Lisa.

Anna went to the fridge and took out a couple of sodas, then headed for the barn. Softly, she approached the open door and peered in, wondering if it was safe yet. Anna heard the lambs clamoring for attention. As she peaked over the fenced partition, she saw Lisa sitting on the straw-littered floor, hugging a lamb to her chest. Lisa dragged the lamb's face away from her head as it tried to nibble at her hair. Tears were streaming down her face, and Anna saw her chest heaving with the effort of keeping the sobs from escaping.

Was it too soon to disturb her? The last thing a fourteen-year-old wanted was to cry in front of her mom or explain her tears.

Anna retreated from the barn, went to the recreation area, and sat down on an Adirondack near the firepit. She cracked open a soda and wondered what she'd say to Lisa. Or not say. Maybe that would be the better answer. She knew that if anyone begrudged her staying back in Olympia, it would be Lisa. Anna massaged her temple as she felt the familiar tingling of an approaching migraine.

Matt was probably right when he said the children wouldn't understand her reasoning. Although in all the conversations they'd had, he'd never mentioned any anger problems. Sadness, yes. Yet even that had dissolved once Chloe had arrived. Well, time to put her Momma's hat on and figure this thing out. She sat quietly, enjoying the serenity of the scene before her, arming herself with patience. She had almost finished her soda when she saw Lisa exit the barn.

"Lisa? I have a soda here if you want one. Come on over and sit with me. Please."

Anna watched Lisa hesitate, her gaze darting around her. What was she nervous about? There was no one close by.

Slowly, Lisa approached her and flopped down on a chair, grabbing the can of soda and popping it. She took two big swallows, then wiped her mouth and let out a huge burp.

Anna smiled. "Good one. Well brought up."

Lisa giggled. "Sodas always make me burp." She met Anna's gaze, then glanced away. Her foot began tapping nervously.

"Having a tough day?"

"Kinda. No big deal." Lisa's voice was still trembling a little, but Anna was glad that she hadn't stood up and walked away from her.

"Once in a while, we all have a crappy day. We're all allowed to get upset now and then. It's a sign that something's bugging us that we have to deal with. And sometimes, it's nothing except frustration, and it doesn't seem so bad the next day."

"I guess so. I've seen you angry. Even if you didn't want to admit that you were angry, we could tell." Lisa was trying to justify her temper by comparing it to her mother's.

"Yes, I remember that. But once your dad and I talked about it and got it out of our systems, we were okay. Right?" Anna reached over and patted her daughter's knee. "You will be too. If you want to talk about it, I'll listen."

"No thanks. Maybe later." Lisa glanced at her mother, her red eyes still swollen from crying. "Growing up sucks, Mom."

"Sometimes it does. And sometimes, it's absolutely wonderful. Remember that." Anna sat quietly, looking around her and letting her daughter have time to process her feelings. When she heard Lisa's breathing return to normal and her foot stop bouncing, she made a suggestion. "I'm going up to the main lodge and help Kari make jam. Why don't you go back home and clean up your room? Put your music on and think about this. See if maybe you might have overreacted about something. I'll be home in an hour or so. We can talk then if you want. Or not. It's up to you, honey. I love you, and I'm so glad I'm home with you."

"Me too, Mom." Lisa stood up and picked up her mom's empty soda can, and headed back home.

Anna watched her progress. Her shuffling steps and stooped shoulders were proof that whatever had happened wasn't so simply dispelled. She could feel her daughter's pain and sighed, relieved she was here to guide her.

She raised her gaze skyward and squinted as the bright light stabbed into her eye socket. Yup. A migraine was coming. *Please, God, give me strength*. She'd find a quiet space at the lodge and close her eyes for a while. No jam, after all.

CHAPTER 9 - YOUNG LOVE

R ay shook his son's shoulder harder this time. "Are you coming or not? Aaron?" Ray threw the bedcovers off him and tapped the back of his head. "Breakfast in five. We leave right after. I'm not keeping Thomas waiting. If you want to fish, get the lead out."

"Yea, yea. I'm coming." Aaron sat and ran his hands over his face and hair. "Is it even light yet? Holy smokes, Dad. Don't fish bite later in the day?"

"Not the big ones. Do you want a tyee or not?" Ray headed into the kitchen. He'd finished making lunches for the four of them, grabbed a Ziploc of cookies and put them in the cooler, then snapped it closed.

Pouring himself another coffee, he waited a minute before taking the eggs and bacon from the fridge. The smell of bacon could bring Aaron from miles away. The kid loved his breakfast.

He filled the pan with thick Applewood smoked bacon and put the burner on medium-high. Scrambled eggs would have to do. He couldn't flip an egg if his life depended on it.

He beat six eggs in a bowl, added a dollop of milk, salt, and pepper, and set it aside.

Aaron shuffled into the kitchen, yawning and rubbing the top of his head. "Can't believe we have to get up at 4 in the morning. The sun's not even up yet."

"For your information, this is called pre-dawn, and soon you'll see a magnificent sunrise. Well worth getting up for."

"I guess so. I'm surprised Mom's not up to see us off."

"We were up late last night, getting our gear and groceries ready. I told her I'd look after making breakfast so she could sleep in." Ray turned the bacon over and lowered the heat. "I thought the smell of bacon might get you moving. Get the bread out and make toast, please."

"Do you want juice, Dad?" Aaron sounded like he was beginning to wake up and anticipate the hardy breakfast.

"Sure, I think we still have orange juice left."

"It's kind of nice going out, just the two of us. Jed and I have fun together, but once in a while, it's good to get away from each other."

"Thomas is bringing Sonja along, and the boat doesn't hold more than four comfortably. Jed will be going with his dad next week. He wasn't upset, was he?"

"No, not at all. Jed said he had other things to do. He's been acting a little weird lately." Aaron shrugged as he poured the juice into glasses and finished setting the table.

"Maybe he just needs time to himself. He's going into grade twelve this year. There are lots for him to think about."

"I know. Uncle Matt wants him to stay another year after he graduates and help around here. Uncle says he could find him a job at Ace Hardware, and Jed could gain some work experience while he waits for me to graduate. Or Jed could work with you when you get an outside job. It's making me feel guilty. You know, like I'm holding Jed back when he wants to go."

"True, that might be bothering him. Although, both your uncle and I would feel better if you two head off to UBC together."

"But Dad, when we came up here, we thought we'd be going back to UW. Then we could hook up with our friends. I don't see why you changed your minds."

"Let's not do this *again*. You know how dangerous it still is in Washington. You're lucky you even get to go to university in Canada. Uncle Matt called in some favors with his Alma Mater, and as long as you pass the SATs, you'll be accepted in Vancouver with dorm accommodations."

"I guess so." A heaping plate of bacon and eggs took over Aaron's attention. Toast and jam afterward finally filled him before he put his dishes in the sink. "Ok, ready to go anytime you are." He grabbed his jean jacket to ward off the early morning chill and opened the door.

"Aaron!" His dad's raised eyebrows and finger-pointing at the cooler brought him back to earth.

"Huh? Oh, yea." Aaron returned and picked up the cooler, and went outside.

Ray followed his son as he lumbered his way to the back of the pickup truck and tied the cooler down on the box to prevent it from sliding around. Ray put their rods, tackle box, and a couple of sleeping bags in the cab.

"Why are we bringing the sleeping bags?" Aaron asked as he jumped in the truck with Ray.

"It's my surprise for you. We'll be overnighting near Bella Bella, so we can go back out early tomorrow for another day of trolling for King Salmon. Depending on the fishing, we may be gone for two nights. We'll be sleeping under the stars tonight at a favorite place Sonja has enjoyed over the years with her dad."

"Wow! That's so cool, Dad. When did you cook up this adventure?"

"Thomas, Matt, and I have been impressed with your work this summer and wanted to reward you with something special. Thomas and Sonja will take Matt and Jed out next weekend for the same trip. See how you boys handle the open ocean. We'll also fish for halibut. If we're lucky enough to hook one on, that will be something. I've heard they're often over a hundred pounds of almost dead weight as they come up. I've never caught one myself, so I'm keeping my fingers crossed."

Twenty minutes later, they pulled into the municipal marina near the ferry terminal. Aaron retrieved the cooler and clattered down the metal grated gang plank towards Thomas' boat. Sonja waved to them and hopped out, allowing them room to stow their gear and cooler. The motors were warming up.

"Hey Thomas, Sonja. Thanks for inviting me along. I can't wait to get out there." Aaron high-fived his friends enthusiastically. "Oops, sorry, Sonja." Sonja waved her hand about, taking the sting away from Aaron's excited greeting.

"That's ok. Now that I know how strong you are, *you're* going to be my assistant." Sonja laughed as she pointed her finger directly at him. "Deal?"

"Deal. Whatever you say, you name it."

"Be prepared then. Today we'll fish Hakaii Pass, an area between Hunter and Calvert Island. When we're ready to call it quits, we'll head into one of the coves and pitch a drop tent and spend the night there. We better catch some fish, or otherwise, we'll only be eating potatoes and carrots roasted in the fire. Unless you're a good clam digger. Then tomorrow, we'll head farther into the Strait and see what we can find."

Aaron was so excited that his questions and chatter soon got on his dad's nerves. "Aaron, enough for a few minutes, will you? Calm down and listen for a while." Ray tapped his son's shoulders as he noticed the surprised look on his face and tried to switch the subject. "Thomas wants you to watch him handle the boat. Pay attention. He might need you to drive while he sets things up for us. You think you can do that?"

"Hell, yea. I mean, yes, of course, I can. I'm a quick study, right Thomas?"

"You are that. Stand beside me. I'll explain the instrument panel as we go along."

"Are you ready for me to untie the moorings yet?" Ray called out.

When Thomas gave a thumbs-up, Ray jumped back on the dock, released the lines, and threw them on board while Sonja held the boat to the pier. Within minutes, 'MissB-haven,' had slipped away into the morning mist.

Sonja and Ray sat on the bench seats at the back of the boat and zipped the windows closed for the time being. They'd open them later when it was warmer and would roll the canvas out of the way for fishing. But for now, it kept them out of the damp morning weather.

"You have a nice son there. You must be proud of him. Thomas tells me he's helped a lot at your place and is very respectful. He says that about Jed too. To me, that says a lot about their parents."

"Thank you. We're a close-knit family, but I have to admit I was worried about how they'd take the move up here. I guess you've heard what we were going through in our home state. Much as we hated to uproot them, we were more worried about what we'd all have to endure by staying there."

"I can't imagine how hard the decision must've been."

"It was. We second-guessed ourselves several times before it was too late to change back. Originally, Matt wanted to keep Safe Haven as a Christian faith-based retreat, but there were drawbacks with the organization that advised us. Eventually, we found out about intentional communities, which made sense to us. We've kept the Christian aspect but expanded the overall goals to include sustainability and low environmental impact. And so far, so good. I'm glad we have a variety of families and age ranges living together. We're still organizing ourselves." Ray's right foot began to bounce as he continued. "I hope no one thinks we're isolationists. Although we've been to several Sunday markets in town, we've been too busy preparing things for our first winter to meet many other families."

"Of course. You needed time to adjust to your new lifestyle. One thing at a time."

"Exactly. I'm glad to see you more often at the Haven. We appreciate your help. That dish you brought at the Mother's Day barbecue was delicious. Kari went foraging for fiddleheads the week after. Hers wasn't as tasty as yours, but she tried. We've missed asparagus since we've moved here. It's so expensive in the grocery store that we hadn't bothered buying it."

"I'm glad you enjoyed my contribution. Mom said she learned it from a night school cooking course featuring First Nations dishes. It's very simple. We just use butter or olive oil, add a pinch of sea salt, and give the fiddleheads a quick stir-fry. Drizzle lemon over them, then slide them onto a platter. Sometimes I add a chopped red pepper or diced tomato or whatever you like to make it more colorful. It makes a healthy and tasty side dish. Next time, I'll bring something different. Dad also taught me how to make sushi. Do any of you like that?"

"Kari and Anna love it. I remember them often going for lunch at a sushi bar. Even Lisa enjoys it as long as it's a California roll—the ones with prawns instead of fish?"

"Usually, that's how people start to enjoy it. Then they get braver and try other kinds of seafood. I can teach you all how to make it one day if you're interested."

"You're on. I'll pass that on to Kari and Anna. They'll probably give you a call to organize something. Will you and Thomas and his family be joining us for Thanksgiving this year? Your family is welcome too. Everybody will bring a dish, and we'll have a buffet in the main lodge."

"Thomas hasn't asked yet, but that sounds great. I'm sure my family would enjoy meeting your community. Sharing a holiday is a good way to make friends."

"Exactly. The thing I notice the most about living here is how much we help each other. City life is lonely compared to this. Families are spread out nowadays, and life is so busy that they hardly stay in touch. Kari and Anna are exceptions, of course, thank God. Most people are lucky to have more than one friendship outside of a work situation. Everyone tends to stick to themselves."

"That's true, even in university. You know the dorm mates on either side of you and the ones you hang with during class. There are very few deep friendships."

"I agree. And it's so peaceful here. Don't get me wrong. It's beautiful in Washington, with all the mountains and ocean and everything. But the public is anxious, nervous. Ever since climate change hit California, Nevada, and Arizona especially, people started moving north. The government hasn't been able to keep up with the demand.

There's not enough housing or services for newcomers, and it's caused a ton of problems. You can't call it peaceful these days. Protests and anxiety are peaking at dangerous levels. This place seems like heaven to us after the past few years."

"So, climate change isn't seen as a hoax anymore? Canadians have been watching the politics in the States for years, wondering if the majority of Americans would ever acknowledge global warming."

"No. Definitely not a hoax. Matt and I had a lot of conversations about how much we kept our heads in the sand. We didn't see how much we abused our earth and what the consequences would be. We did what we wanted, when we wanted, with no consideration to anyone but our immediate families. Then we justified it, calling it progress. Now, look where most people are." Ray leaned his forearms on his knees and stared downwards, shaking his head.

"Don't worry too much, Ray. You weren't the only ones. Canadians aren't blameless either. Look at the Suncor and Syncrude companies in Alberta, extracting oil from the tar sands. Then we talk about how we need the tax dollars for healthcare and education, so we turn a blind eye to the pollution it creates throughout the world."

Sonja shook her head as she pondered the dilemma. "You know, one day, I'd like to take you and your family along the Atnarko River and show you the Hunlen Falls dropping 850 feet into it. The sheer cliffs that divide one super terrain to the coastal one are mind-boggling. That happened in the Jurassic Age for crying out loud. Yet, in less than a few hundred years, humans have changed the natural course of our earth. It's scary. No wonder we sometimes choose to ignore it."

"That's one of our governing laws at Safe Haven, to be environmentally conscious. No chemical fertilizers. We use solar-generated power whenever we can and practice cooperative living. We want to keep thinking of ways to do our part and stay safe. We're small potatoes. But it has to start somewhere. What we're doing here is also being done in small communities throughout the world. I hope it's not too late."

"I hear you. I think the point is we need to pay attention to every decision we make and how it affects everything around us." Sonja blew out a breath of despair, then pulled her shoulders back. "But on the positive side, I believe that science and technology will find a way to neutralize the damage we've done, and we'll find our way back."

"But why do we have to wait until the last minute? What if it doesn't work that way this time?"

"I know, that's a scary thought. We'll have to concentrate on individual efforts and technology to correct our mistakes. If enough people start the process, we might turn this around. But today, we're going to enjoy nature and count our blessings and hopefully catch our dinner."

"I sure hope you're right on both points. That's why we came up here." Ray rubbed the back of his neck as he tried to come to terms with the new reality. As he felt the boat slow, gearing down to almost neutral, he moved towards the front of the boat.

"Thomas? What's going on? Do you need help?" Looking out the side windows, he tried to determine what was happening.

"Nope. I just thought we'd drift here for a bit. Take a look along the shoreline there, by the mouth of the creek. See them?"

Aaron pointed as he saw the movement. "There, Dad. A mama grizzly bear and her cubs. Awesome!" Aaron ran to the back and zipped open the windows for a clear look. He leaned out, stretching as far as he could.

Sonja smiled as she passed him the binoculars for an up-close view and listened to his declarations of awe. She was probably used to scenes like these. For Ray, they never failed to make him grateful for his eyesight and for the opportunity to witness nature's glory. It was a bonus to witness someone like his son seeing it all for the first time.

The foursome sat quietly, passing the binoculars to each other as they watched mama bear surge into the creek, fishing for returning salmon. A mighty swipe sent a salmon to the beach, and then she returned to the creek's edge. The cubs pranced about, the fish flapping frantically to find its way back to the water.

Again, mama bear eyed the waters carefully then crouched before leaping into the stream, trapping their next meal. As the mama bear's nose dove in, she withdrew a salmon between her jaws. She lumbered out of the creek and dropped it on the rocks, where she placed a giant paw atop it, then ripped it apart. The cubs came near, mewling for scraps.

"Watch the skies, Aaron," Sonja advised.

As they looked above, several bald eagles sat in the tree tops eyeing the meal below, while one circled safely above the bears, screeching for them to leave.

"Once the bears depart, they'll land and scavenge the leftovers. Nothing will go to waste."

"Awesome. Dad? Have you got your cell phone? Can you zoom in and take pics of that? Mom will go crazy seeing this. You know her."

"Yes, she'll be envious that she didn't get to come. Alright, but I'll only take a few. I forgot to bring a charger, and I'll need to save some battery life for our fishing trip."

"Darn! Ok, forget it. Maybe you should skip this—I'll need proof of my trophy fish."

"No, I'll take a couple of shots to remember this. We'll just have to be careful." Aaron's reasoning amused Ray. Aaron wanted proof of his catch, no matter what else happened. Such was youth. Their perspective was still narrow.

JED WAS LOADING the ATV with his knapsack filled with drinks and food. He rolled their towels up and tied them down into the carrier while he waited for Chloe to join him.

He felt strange leaving his sister behind, but with Aaron gone, there was no way both Lisa and Chloe could come. Lisa left in a huff, angry as all get out, but what could he do? He couldn't carry two of them on the seat behind him.

Maybe he should've just canceled the ride to their swimming hole. But Chloe looked so disappointed when he suggested it. Whatever Chloe said to Lisa must have been a doozer because his sister seldom lost her temper enough to screech in frustration and stomp across the fields.

"Is everything alright?" Jed watched her sister tear toward home, her arms swinging angrily.

Chloe had a surprised expression on her face, probably similar to his.

"I think so. Lisa's been moody lately. I don't know what her problem is, but you're right. You can't very well take both of us. I'm glad you didn't cancel because I was itching to get out of here."

"Tomorrow, I'll take Lisa on my own to make up for today. Dad told me Aaron would spend a night or two away, so I'm not sure exactly when he'll be back. Lucky bugger."

"How come you didn't get to go? I thought you loved fishing?"

"I'm going next week with my dad, and we'll be making the same trip. We'll overnight close to Bella Bella so we can save the travel time and fish in the Strait. I wonder how Uncle Ray and Aaron are doing. Uncle gets seasick pretty easily in rolling waves. I hope he brought Gravol along." Jed snickered, then motioned for Chloe to hop onboard. "Have you got everything?"

"I have my bathing suit underneath my clothes and lunch in my backpack. You already have my towel. That's enough, isn't it?"

"Should be. We're only going for the afternoon. I told my mom we'd be home by six for supper. We'll follow the river up to Snootli Creek campground."

"Sounds good, let's go. I don't want to waste any time." Chloe slapped the helmet on her head and waited for him to hop on.

After they left their community, Jed increased the speed, making Chloe giggle and hang on tighter.

Jed knew he was tempting fate. As she pressed herself against his back, it brought back the memory of her breasts trying to escape the confines of her bathing suit on their last excursion to Snootli Creek. That incident had woken him up more times than he'd like to admit. Taking Chloe swimming alone today would be a test for both of them.

Frequently shirtless like his father and uncle, both Aaron and Jed were becoming muscular young men. Jed couldn't help be proud when he caught Chloe staring at him then blushing when she caught his eye. She'd turn away and resume whatever chores she'd been working on. Lisa would often glance over at him and frown, wondering what was going on.

Today, he'd need every bit of self-control to bury his feelings. As long as he didn't act on them, he'd be OK. Jed wondered if she knew her effect on him.

God, give me the strength to resist temptation.

Crossing the many creeks that drained the mountains to the Bella Coola River helped take Jed's mind off the attraction and focus on the land around them. Jed slipped into his role of a savvy guide, having traveled the trails with his dad or Thomas probably a hundred times since they'd first come here. Jed and Chloe stopped when he spied points of interest or deer grazing almost hidden in the woods. His dad made sure he could identify the mountains and use the GPS, so if they got lost, he could always show Chloe how to use the two-way radio and let rescuers know where they were.

Now Jed was teaching Chloe.

ONCE THEY PASSED the small airport that serviced Bella Coola, Jed followed the river further east until they reached a sandy stretch with deeper blue pools. He parked the ATV and checked the shoreline. Thomas had warned him to look for spawning salmon on the beach. If the cycle had started and carcasses appeared, he and Chloe needed to move on and find another area. The smell of the carrion drew bears, and it wasn't wise to get between a bear and his food supply. Uncle Ray had told them all about the scare he and Aunt Kari had when they went swimming one evening last week.

Jed sighed with relief. The cycle hadn't started yet. Next week school would be starting, which also heralded the salmon spawn, but the breeding cycle could start earlier or later. This spot would be good, not a person in sight.

"I brought a foldup bamboo mat to use. We'll save our towels for drying ourselves." Jed removed the mat from the carrier and spread it on the beach, anchoring the four corners with rocks. He pulled out his towel and rolled it up as a pillow, and threw it on the mat.

Chloe followed suit.

Jed pulled off his T-shirt and jeans. Tying his bathing trunks tighter, he sprinted to the water, splashed to knee depth, then did a shallow dive. "Woo-hoo! I beat you, Chloe." He floated on his back, holding himself in place with arm movements. Looking up at the bright sky surrounded by icy mountain tips, he sighed with contentment.

God, he loved it here. When he thought of what he'd be doing in his hometown right now, Jed knew he wouldn't exchange this for any of that. Summertime in Olympia had been hanging with his friends, playing ball, and trying to meet new girls. He missed his friends for sure, but not as much as he thought he would.

This lifestyle was a real adventure every day, and he enjoyed how spontaneous they could be. Yes, they had jobs to do, responsibilities they had to manage. But they were learning so much. And afterward, they had the freedom to explore.

He turned his head as he heard Chloe squeal as she tiptoed in the water. She had a pair of short-shorts on and a hot pink halter top. Not really a bathing suit, but holy crow!

Jed gasped and sputtered as he swallowed water when he lost focus on staying afloat. For her age, Chloe could sure fill out that combination. Jed trod water, waiting for her to catch up with him.

Chloe submerged herself, then swam underwater towards Jed, coming up only an arm's length away from him.

He could see her long legs gliding and her arms using the breast stroke to get to him. Suddenly he felt a twinge inside his trunks. Oh no!

As she surfaced and treaded water, she lunged her head backward to dip her hair out of her face, then wiped the beads of water from her pink cheeks. Her blue eyes sparkled as she splashed him right smack in the face.

Game on! Jed splashed her back, then dove underwater to grab her legs together and push her backward.

She lost her balance and came up gurgling with laughter. "Not fair! You're stronger than I am." She sprayed him again, then darted away, swimming towards the shallower section.

"Want to try handstands again?" Jed suggested.

"Sure. I'll bet I'm better now. I've been doing handstands in my bedroom. I can go up and down slowly now, with my legs together. If we had a competition, I'd bet I'd get higher marks than you." Her playful smile teased Jed in a way he hadn't expected.

"Ok, show off, let's see your stuff." Jed crossed his arms and dared her to start. "C'mon, let's see how good you are. Do you need a lift to get you going?"

"No-o-o." Chloe stared at Jed's mocking stance before sucking in a deep breath to set herself up. She tried to get her legs up, but they came down quickly. She tried again.

Jed tapped her shoulder. "You're too shallow. Move to deeper water, and then the natural buoyancy will help you get your legs up."

"Never thought of that. Ok." Chloe edged out a little deeper, looking for a rock she could hang onto like an anchor when she lifted her legs. She took a deep breath and positioned herself, then slowly lifted her legs out of the water.

Jed counted to three before Chloe lowered her legs and popped up giggling.

"See! I told you I could do it."

"Fluke. Do it again," Jed taunted with a grin.

Again, Chloe took a deep breath, but this time she kicked up her legs too quickly.

Uh-oh. Jed realized she'd probably end up going completely backward. He instinctively clasped her thighs to steady her.

She gasped and shook herself loose from his touch. She lurched up, coughing and burping.

"Oops, did I make you swallow water? I was just trying to help you stay up." Jed patted her back, hoping to relieve her coughing spasm.

Chloe let out another loud belch and began laughing, which was such a relief that Jed joined in.

He reached over and pulled a strand of hair away from her cheek, then stilled. Chloe's skin was so perfectly soft and pretty that Jed couldn't take his hand away. He searched her eyes and saw the jump of interest in them as he bent to kiss her cheek.

Chloe leaned towards him, placing her hand on his chest. She looked up at him, and he hoped what he saw was the result of all the secret glances they had been sending each other for weeks. He tugged her closer to him and pressed his lips to hers.

Ahh. Softer than Jed imagined, sweeter than he hoped. He felt her breasts push into his chest as Chloe held onto him tightly, inviting him to continue. He kissed her again and again, short, feathery kisses before finally breaking away. Jed kissed her forehead and closed his eyes. Gently he pulled himself out of the embrace and stared into Chloe's stormy blue eyes, filled with as much passion as he imagined his held.

"Wow. We've been dancing around this for a while. You're beautiful, Chloe."

"I've thought about you a lot and wondered if we'd ever kiss like this. I'm glad we're alone today." She grabbed Jed's hand and placed it above the swell of her breast. "Feel that? My heart's pounding. I'm so happy you like me too. I wasn't sure."

"I've been trying to ignore my feelings. You're too young for me, Chloe. You're what? Fifteen?"

"Yes, so what? Don't tell me we're not allowed to date each other or be with each other."

"Actually, that's exactly what I'm telling you. Uncle Ray noticed the looks we've been giving each other. He asked me if anything was going on, and I told him he was wrong about us. I'll be going to university next year, and it wouldn't be fair to become involved now. It would make it too hard for both of us when I leave."

"Really? You're assuming that this attraction we have would end up with us sleeping together. I like you, but I'm not stupid. I have plans for the future too." Chloe's voice shook as she tried to explain herself and backed away from him. "So, now what? I like you. I like kissing you. I like talking with you and exploring with you."

"I know. Same here. We can still do that, Chloe, but we can't do *this* anymore. You know what this could lead to, and it wouldn't take much, believe me. My parents and yours would have a fit. I'm hoping to go to university soon. I can't get seriously involved with anyone, let alone you."

Chloe gave him a dirty look, one he probably deserved, then splashed her way out of the water. She grabbed her towel and wrapped it around her but kept her back to him.

Jed saw her shoulders shaking. Damn. He'd made her cry.

He went to her and put a hand on her shoulder. "Chloe, honey, I'm sorry. I really am. I thought I wouldn't act on my feelings. I'm sorry."

Chloe turned around, lifting her eyes to him, the tears still evident. She raised her hands and grabbed his face, forcing it down to her lips, kissing him passionately. Then, abruptly, she let go. "I'm sorry too. Think about what you'll be missing. Good thing school starts next week. I'll need to find someone to replace you."

Her declaration rocked him.

Chloe glared at him for a moment, probably watching the shock in his eyes or on his face. Then she gathered her towel in a huff and stomped down the beach to another sandy spot. Spreading the towel out, she laid on her stomach and ignored him.

Jed laid on the bamboo mat and shaded his eyes with his arm as he scolded himself. He should've known this was bound to happen. As long as it was the four of them together, they ignored the growing feelings between them. Uncle Ray was right. Maybe in another life, they'd have come together, but not in this situation.

It was just a summer flirtation, that was all. One that had to be nipped in the bud. He thought of the verses in the bible, the sermons about the dangers of flirtation, and knew he needed to be strong. *Please, God, help me do the right thing.* She was way too young, and they needed to be smart. If there were genuine, romantic feelings between them, they'd still be there in a few years. He sat up and glanced over towards Chloe, who was still baking in the sun.

"Hey, Chloe! Are you hungry? I'm going to grab my lunch. Come and sit with me."

"Not yet. Maybe later."

She hadn't turned her head to look at him, so her voice was muffled. Jed couldn't tell if she was still crying or not. Maybe she just needed time. He went to the ATV, grabbed both their knapsacks, and dropped hers next to her beach towel. "Ok, well, here's your bag. You might want to put sunscreen on too. You're turning pink." He waited for a response, but obviously, she was still pouting.

Jed shrugged and returned to his mat, taking out his soda and sandwiches and devouring them. He laid down again, wondering what his next step should be. Soon Jed dozed off, not waking until he heard water splashing nearby. He sat up, thankful to see Chloe in the water, cooling off. Jed debated joining her then decided it was wiser not to.

Chloe walked out of the water, twisting the water from her long hair. She returned to her towel and picked up her knapsack, then came to sit beside Jed. Chloe rummaged through and found her container of fruit salad and a fork. "Want any?" she offered.

"No, thanks. I'm full. Are we okay now? Can we go back to the way we were? Please?"

Chloe saw the anguish in his eyes and guessed he was feeling guilty. "I guess so. It's going to be hard to forget those kisses, though." She jabbed a piece of watermelon and slurped its juices. "You're right. It'd be too complicated. Sneaking around." She ate a few more pieces of fruit before putting her lunch down. "You know your sister had a big mad on. She accused me of having a crush on you. Lisa said she saw the way you looked at me too. She warned me we were tempting fate."

"Hmm. I never thought Lisa was so observant. I guess my sister's more mature than I gave her credit. Do you think that's why she was so mad when she left us this afternoon?"

"Yup. She knew we were taking chances being by ourselves. And she was right."

"Are you going to tell her we kissed?" Jed frowned as he stared at Chloe, wondering what kind of shitstorm that would produce.

"No, I don't think so. That might make Lisa tell your parents and blow this thing way out of whack. What do you think? I know we're supposed to be honest, but I don't have problems with little white lies. The truth might cause us both a lot of grief."

"Exactly. No kisses. Just friends, swimming and having lunch and trail riding. Right?"

"Yes. You can trust me. We just swam and horsed around. End of story."

"Right. Thanks, Chloe. I'm older. I'll be more careful from now on. We're just friends. Good friends."

Chloe punched him in the upper arm. "Best friends." Her eyebrows waggled up and down as they both broke down laughing in relief.

CHAPTER 10 - FINDING THE
MEANING OF INTENTION

In comparison to other families, Nathan and Brianna Cameron carried a heavy load. They cheerfully honored their commitment to paying rent plus working at least two days a week around the community. Whether it was yard maintenance, animal care, or vegetable gardening, they were enthusiastic and energetic helpers, while their children were their pride and joy alongside them.

Yet, their focus of joining Safe Haven was to work in the field at least three days a week on his research grant. In mid-July, Nathan and Brianna had brought up their problem at the last board meeting when Matt announced open discussion time. Nathan spoke of the dilemma that he and Brianna were experiencing.

"We're not sure how to handle this." Nathan had tapped his pencil on the paperwork in front of him. He glanced at his wife, who nodded encouragement. "You all know that we've committed to being here for a minimum of two years, which I thought would give us time to assess the scope involved. We just didn't realize how big an area this is.

Seeing it on a map doesn't help you realize how much time it takes to get to certain locations."

Nathan glanced around him, looking at their concerned expressions, and took a drink of water, and cleared his throat. "Our day trips have been great. Both the boys love to spend time with a reliable and fun babysitter like Lisa. Our explorations are less stressful because we know she can get help with our boys from any of you if she has problems. That's a huge relief for us. It's brought home the old saying, 'it takes a village to raise a child.' Brianna and I feel very fortunate to have found all of you."

Nathan opened his mouth to continue, then closed it and stared straight ahead, frowning. "I've been trying to ignore the problem of travel time and the kids, but I can't anymore. I have to find a solution for covering the extensive territory my thesis calls for." He continued to explain the isolated areas they needed to access for research on his microbiology thesis, and their day trips weren't sufficient.

To get the statistics they needed in remote locations, they needed to take advantage of the long summer and fall days. They realized the most efficient use of their time would be to base camp overnight, or maybe even two nights. That way, they could record the GPS coordinates with the slides Nathan collected, and Brianna could photograph the required visual proof. They would postpone analyzing the information until the winter to sort and catalog the samples and prepare his written paper. They just couldn't figure out how to manage the overnight expeditions. After listening to their dilemma, the group discussed ways in which they could help.

WHEN THEY BROKE FOR COFFEE, Gwen pulled Mark aside. "They have such sweet children. It's been a joy to have both the little ones and the teenagers around us. Life's interesting again. I'd given up hope of being part of a family. Now, look where we are." Gwen's eyes misted as she felt the happiness in her heart whenever the kids were near. "Every time I'm on the porch on my rocker, Troy always comes to say hi. He climbs up on my lap without blinking an eye. He loves to cuddle and show me his newest find. So, I generally shoo Lisa away for a break and give him all my attention."

"I know the feeling. Tyler's always full of questions, and he likes to tag behind me whenever I'm near the barn. He never stops talking. Honestly, I feel ten years younger since we've come here." Mark smiled as he sipped his hot coffee. "I'm enjoying it too—it's almost as if we're their grandparents."

"Which gives me an idea. Why don't we volunteer to take the boys for the overnights? It would certainly help Nathan and Brianna, and we'd get to pretend they're our grandchildren. What do you think?" The words tumbled over each other as Gwen searched her husband's face for his response.

When she saw his eyes light up, she knew she was right. Those kids had found their way into his heart, too.

"We'd need help, honey. We're not spring chickens. I don't think I could keep up with them all day, then enjoy the evenings with them too."

"I understand. I'd like to suggest the possibility, though. Let's see what we can come up with." Gwen leaned over and bussed him on the cheek. "I do believe this will be a good move for both of us. We can do a trial run and decide whether it would work. Do you want to give it a shot?"

"Sure, why not. Just be careful not to get too attached."

Mark squeezed her hands as he stared straight into her eyes. "We don't need any more broken hearts. Their project is a temporary situation, and you'll need to remember that."

The sound of Matt knocking on the table brought them all back to resume business.

"We've all had time to think about the Camerons' predicament. Does anyone have any suggestions?" Matt looked around the table. When his eyes landed on Gwen's smile, he returned it. "Go ahead, Gwen. What are you thinking about?"

"Mark and I were just talking about how much we enjoy your boys, Nathan. We may be too old to look after them all day, but if you have someone for the day, we could relieve them for suppertime and put them to bed in our spare room. Then Lisa or someone else could pick them up after breakfast. Would that work?"

"Are you sure?" Brianna piped in. "It seems like a lot of trouble for you two. The boys talk about you a lot. I think they'd get a kick out of having sleepovers at your place. I know that won't be a problem for us, but I don't want it to be too stressful for you two."

"You'll only be gone two nights max, and Lisa can babysit until September. Maybe someone else can take over when school starts. Why don't we give it a try and see how we feel about it? Within a few trips, we'll know if we can handle it and whether the boys enjoy it." Gwen lifted her hands in the air. "There's nothing to lose by giving it a try. We'll both be honest about it. If it doesn't work, we'll figure something else out." Gwen searched Nathan for his reaction.

He was letting out a breath slowly, and the frown that had wrinkled his forehead was easing.

Matt scrutinized the two couples, giving them a minute

to consider the proposition. "That's a very generous offer, Gwen. Let's not jump to solutions, though. Why don't both of you think about this, then get together privately and make your decision?"

"That's a great idea." Kari jumped in. "Gwen and Mark have become like grandparents for all the kids. This arrangement sounds like it would work well for both sides. And I'll be teaching Tyler and Troy in September, so I'll take over babysitting from Lisa until it's time for them to go to Gwen and Mark's. After all, it's not every day. A couple of days a week doesn't interrupt anyone for long, and if it helps you guys out, then why not?"

"I hate to bother all of you about our kids. But it's either finding a solution within Safe Haven or looking for a nanny from town. And we don't expect this caregiving to be free. We can afford to pay for our children's care. The university has invested a lot of money into me, and I have to give them my best effort. That's why I've turned to you to get suggestions." Nathan looked at the faces around the table, then looked down and slowly smiled. He seemed to be struggling for words, choked up with emotion. "I'm not used to asking for help."

"No problem, Nathan. You and Brianna are part of this family. That's why we joined an intentional community. We help each other out so we can live the life that's essential to us. Your kids are important, your research is important, and you've shown your commitment to the rest of us too. Everyone here has a priority they want to embrace, but it's easier to do when we can help each other. Money doesn't have to enter into this, but that's between you and whoever your caregivers will be."

Gwen interrupted. "Mark and I are so very grateful to be here. We weren't sure if our decision was right, but it didn't take long to recognize it was perfect for us. We want to share our lives with all of you too. We don't have children or grandchildren, but neither one of us feels alone anymore. Let us help with this." Gwen clasped her hand in her husband's, then addressed the Camerons. "How about you and Brianna come over after supper with the kids for a campfire soon? I think we can help each other out."

"Alright, we will. I'll pop over tomorrow to arrange something if that's ok?"

As the meeting drew to a close, there was a positive note in the air. Matt led the attendees in a prayer of thanks, then walked about, shaking everyone's hand. The members put their mugs and plates into the dishwasher, tidied up, then returned home.

A MONTH LATER, Mark finished helping Ray filet the salmon that he and Aaron brought home. Tomorrow they'd start the process of soaking half of the salmon in two different brines for smoking, and the other half would be canned. The halibut was already vacuum-packed and frozen. He'd whip home and take a quick shower before the boys arrived for dinner.

Knowing that Gwen had made double chocolate chip cookies this morning for Tyler and Troy, he needed to lend a hand as she prepared lasagna for their dinner tonight. He'd take the boys to the park and play catch with them. When they called him Papa Mark, it filled his heart with joy. Seeing their smiles and excitement made him feel like a real grandparent, something he'd never thought he'd experience. The highlight of their weeks had quickly become the nights that the Camerons left the boys for an overnight exploration. Mark hadn't seen his wife so happy in years.

Surrounded by friends and adopted family, Mark and Gwen thanked God for the opportunity to join this community. Life had a new meaning for them. Grace was said every night at the dinner table, a welcome habit that showed their gratitude.

ANNA STRAIGHTENED UP, stretching her back and rolling her shoulders as she took time for a short break. Looking around her, she saw Lisa and Chloe leading the lambs to pasture with the sheep. Whatever had happened between the two girls seemed to have been resolved, reassuring Anna that it had been nothing serious.

Anna was tossing mulch over the carrots and beets to help winter better, preferring to be outside gardening than inside preserving. Besides, Pete needed an extra hand as Denyse had joined the preserving side of the harvest. She often saw Mike helping his dad, working side by side, but his attention and aptitude for gardening weren't there at thirteen years old. Mike never lasted longer than an hour or so, but it was probably his cheerful presence that gave Pete the most benefit. Then he'd be gone, following Aaron and Jed around, and helping them with their chores. The older boys had adopted Mike and enjoyed teasing one another as they worked together.

Listening to the two young Cameron boys fussing over Gwen made Anna smile. Tyler and Troy had recently started calling her Nana Gwen. The spry, salt and pepper topped woman played a game of ladders with the boys, throwing a rope with a golf ball at each end towards the three-rung ladder. When she tossed her last rope, she hit the three-point rung and came up the winner, shouting in triumph. Simply watching them excited to share each other's company made her heart swell with warmth. They all looked so joyful. She was glad that Matt had decided to diversify the ages of the families that would comprise Safe Haven.

There was no doubt about the benefits it provided. The little ones gave the older members unconditional love and joy that they sorely needed. The seniors gave the younger members and children undivided attention and wisdom to anyone who came to visit them. Mutual respect.

She hadn't thought it would go so smoothly. Matt was a born leader. She'd had her doubts, but not anymore. Thank you, Lord.

Their haven was a beehive of activity since she'd arrived. Anna hadn't understood the extent that intentional living would have on all of them. To say she was pleasantly surprised would be an understatement. If Leanne and Fiona could see her now, they wouldn't believe it. Even she was astonished at how quickly her outside world had faded from everyday life. Anna felt a physical connection to each family in the community and could also feel their affection for her. It was as if her world had shrunk to this idyllic location, and at this point, she welcomed it. For how long it would satisfy her, she had no idea. One day at a time became her mantra.

Two short whistles blew, which brought everyone's attention to the picnic area, where Kari stood with a tray of food. Anna grinned at the sight of her sister, always meeting the challenge of feeding the working crew. She removed her gloves and wiped her sweaty hands on her jeans as she walked to meet Kari.

"Just in time. I was getting thirsty. What've you made today?"

"Hi, Anna. Denyse is following with a jug of iced tea and another of water. I've made cream cheese and veggie sandwiches, as well as ham. Take your pick. Sonja arrived a few hours ago to help us. She'll be bringing cookies for dessert soon. I've learned not to bring them at the same time as the sandwiches, or the kids will pig out on that first."

"Sit down and keep me company. How's it going in the lodge? Knowing you and Vera, you have a production line going."

Kari giggled. "We do. Vera's keeping track of everything we're producing. The storage shelves that Ray made for our items are almost full. I think we'll have to add at least another row of shelves to get the last items in, probably in the crafting room for now until we start distributing." Kari leaned over and wiped a smudge off her sister's face, prompting her to giggle again. "Never thought I'd see the day that you'd volunteer for gardening duties."

"Neither did I. I don't know how long it will last, but it feels good to work at something physical. All the reports and studies I've done in the last six months must have fried my brain. Right now, this is exactly the right thing for me, but I know it won't last forever."

"I'll bet it doesn't either. So, what have you got up your sleeve? Come on, I know you. You always have a backup plan." Kari tilted her head towards her sister and smiled as she poured them a glass of iced tea. "Spill the beans. You know you want to."

Anna chuckled. "You know me too well. I've been researching the BC Health Link website. They're accepting resumes and profiles for professionals to man their 8-1-1 site. Have you heard of telenursing?"

"No, not at all. Thomas recommended Dr. Nelson, who's thorough and friendly. But, sometimes it takes a week or two to get an appointment."

"Exactly. In northern or isolated areas like here, people can access non-emergency health care by calling 8-1-1 or visiting their website. Anyone can access nurses for a no-charge symptoms check 24/7. If you don't know who you should be speaking to, they have a 'navigator' who can help you contact a more specific health provider you need."

"Awesome! I've never heard of it. Have you talked to Matt about this idea?"

"No. I thought I'd wait until things slow down around here, like maybe December or January. Last year, I wrote my exams to be certified in Canada, so all I have to do is create a resume and profile with my registration number. Once they do a background check, they'll contact me, and we'll figure out what's available and what type of employment I want." Anna shrugged her shoulders. "I don't know how open they are to part-time nurses, but I'm hoping I can keep my hand in nursing while I'm up here."

"That sounds like a good fit for you. Ray mentioned that Matt's beginning to miss using his professional skills too. There's already a dentist in Bella Coola, so he's been thinking about a different location."

"Yes, in fact, that's what has me thinking about options too. Matt has all his credentials to open a specialist endodontic practice. If he goes to Kitimat or Williams Lake, he could make it similar to a satellite practice and only open one week a month. Most people have to travel to Prince George or Vancouver to get those types of services, so he'd probably acquire a lot of referrals from the small interior towns."

"Hmm. Ray didn't mention anything about that. I guess

he'd fly to his office then? It makes sense. You've told me it's a very lucrative field, and I know he's been a little worried about how much this place has cost so far."

"It would ease the financial part, that's for sure. But it's more that Matt loves his work. He misses it. Anyway, nothing's decided, but it's an option for the future."

"Yea, I can believe it got you motivated too. Well, time will tell. If we can live here and follow our professional paths, that would be the best solution, wouldn't it?"

"Maybe. It keeps the brain stimulated and our skills current. So, we'll see. There are things we'll have to change regarding the availability of the internet. We thought we could live with limited access, but I think we'll be changing our viewpoint on at least some of that. I can see living without TV or streaming services, but Matt's starting to see it's vitally important to have internet communication access in our homes. Meanwhile, I'll concentrate on being here for Matt and our kids. Even though it was my choice to stay behind, I felt a lot of guilt for not being around when my family needed me. Once things slow down, I might volunteer at the high school until the telenursing option becomes available. Sonja says they can always use the extra help."

"True. I'm looking forward to teaching Tyler and Troy in the fall. The older kids are anxious to go back to school next week. It's going to be a lot quieter around here. Aaron's been discussing electives with his dad, trying to figure out what he should major in. It's starting to sink in with Jed's graduation coming up next June, that they'll soon be on their own."

"I know. Jed's been bucking his dad lately. He doesn't want to wait for Aaron to finish his grade twelve. He wants to go straight into university in September."

"I'll bet that's a recipe for a few arguments." Kari slanted her head to one side, searching for her sister's opinion.

"There's been a few heated discussions, nothing serious, though. I'd feel better if Jed was rooming with Aaron or someone we know. I've talked to Pete recently about that. He and Denyse know so many staff and students, he's going to make inquiries. If he can find a solid match for Jed with someone with our set of values, he'll let us know. Then we'll discuss the options. With Jed attending in Vancouver, at least we won't have to worry about the political and social unrest that we would've seen in Washington."

"But don't you worry that Jed could be lured to cross the border to visit his friends, or maybe even stay there? Without having Aaron beside him, I'm sure that would be a temptation."

"We're not giving him his passport, so even if he wanted to, he couldn't go past the border. I'm sure we'll get accused of not trusting him, but we didn't move up here for him to put himself in danger by returning to Olympia."

"Good idea. I'm sure we'll figure this out before Jed graduates. I think it'll be a good idea for him to get away from here soon. I hate to worry, but both Ray and I have noticed that Chloe and Jed seem to exchange some pretty heated glances lately."

"Hmm. Well, they're teenagers, so it's not unexpected. I think once school starts, though, there will be other distractions to diffuse that. I hope so anyway. Thanks for the heads up. I'll keep an eye on things around here."

Anna sighed, and drum rolled her fingers on the table. She caught Kari assessing her and shrugged her shoulder. "Don't worry. We'll work it out."

Anna changed the subject by reaching out for a veggie sandwich piled high with cucumber, tomato, and lettuce on Kari's herbed cream cheese. She bit into the freshly baked bread and groaned with delight. "My goodness, Kari. That's delicious. Can you pour me another iced tea?"

A mixture of deep rambunctious chatter and light-hearted giggles made Anna turn around. Speak of the devils, the kids had arrived for their lunch. Anna kept an eye on the body language, and although Jed and Chloe made sure to keep people in between them, they were darting glances at each other, then looking away.

Sonja arrived bearing cookies and went straight to the teenagers, who each picked three or four before bringing the platter to the picnic table.

"Hey, Sonja. Nice to see you. I'm surprised you're here when school is so close. I thought you'd be busy setting up your schedule for the first week."

"Nice to see you too. But nah, I've learned to be organized. I've learned to save my class lessons from previous years on my computer, then choose from that. Things have changed since we were in high school. Teachers carry their laptops from class to class and follow the topic of interest they decide to deal with each week. Either I email the class their assignments, or I can send the info for printing in the office, then send a student to pick it up and pass them out. I have it set up that the fall timetable is pretty flexible, so I don't get stressed so easily." Sonja passed the cookies to Anna. "Try the oatmeal-coconut. They're so-o good."

Anna eyed the selection and took one of those and a gingersnap. "Smart girl. So how are you and Thomas doing? Matt told me you've been going together for a few years. Any wedding bells on the horizon?"

High-pitched squeals demanding cookies broke into their conversation as Tyler and Troy ran to the picnic table. "I want two of those and two of those," shouted the youngest.

Nana Gwen soon hushed the boys. "Manners, boys. No shouting at the table. Go and wash your hands in the barn and come back here." Gwen sat down beside Sonja, a little out of breath from chasing her wards up the hillside towards the table. "Those two keep me on my toes. Do you know I've lost four pounds without even trying since I've started helping the family out?"

Anna grinned. "Yup, not hard to believe at all. Kids that age keep you busy, that's for sure. You look energized and healthy, though. Are you still happy to have volunteered?"

"No two ways about it. Mark's just as happy as I am. They've given us a new lease on life. We've never been happier." Gwen smiled and smacked her hands on her thighs. "Guess I'd better get washed up to handle the food." She walked towards the barn.

"Gwen was born to be a grandma. Look at how she glows. Thomas loves those two pint-sized hurricanes too. He's always talking about them." Sonja had her eyes on the two ruffians heading their way, waving clean hands in anticipation of cookies.

"We've noticed he's great with kids, even our teenagers. How do you feel about having a family one day?" Anna asked.

"I like kids. Otherwise, I wouldn't be a teacher. Just not sure that I'm ready to have any yet." Sonja lifted her eyebrows as she scanned Anna, probably looking for clues about what Anna knew of their situation. "Has Thomas said anything to you or Matt?"

"No, not at all. Why?" Anna returned her gaze, puzzled at the uneasiness emanating from her question.

"Just wondering."

Anna saw Sonja's fingers tapping quickly on her thighs and knew something was bothering her. "You don't need to worry that you're discussed here. Thomas is very discreet. You never hear him telling stories about anybody. Nobody around here does. We're cautious about maintaining our personal opinions private unless our views are asked for. And even those are kept confidential between the people involved. Gossip is a sure-fire way to kill a small community like ours, so we avoid it."

Watching Sonja's eyes dart between the two boys and Gwen, Anna wondered what had prompted the comment. "You know, I'm sure you have lots of friends and family in town, but if you ever need to chat, you can call me anytime. You can trust that whatever you say won't go anywhere else. My lips are sealed."

"Thanks, Anna. I'm fine. But sometimes, it's nice to bounce ideas off someone who isn't personally involved. You could be my therapist. What do you think about that?"

"That could be a great way to swap services. We have teenagers here that might need guidance at school. Maybe, we could help each other out." Anna brightened when she saw Sonja sigh as if a difficult decision had been resolved.

Maybe she did need a confidant.

After taking a bite from her gingersnap, Anna stood up. "Call me sometime. I'd better get back to work." Anna took the final drink of her iced tea, then returned her soiled utensils to the kitchen tote. She waved to Sonja, then glanced over at her sister and nodded, mouthing her thanks.

Passing by the teenagers, Anna stopped to chat before going back to her garden. Uh-oh. Kari was right. She'd have to talk to Matt and figure out a discreet way to diffuse a potentially tricky situation from developing. Maybe she'd be reaching out to Sonja sooner than she thought. Sometimes it was easier for teenagers to talk honestly with a family friend than with their parents.

Anna looked over her shoulder and saw Sonja pushing the cookies away from Tyler and Troy, obviously stepping in to curb their want for sweets. It didn't take a rocket scientist to see that the boys were using their wily ways and charming smiles to change her mind. Amused, Anna saw Nana Gwen approach with a stern expression on her face and a plateful of sandwiches. Sonja fitted into their community with ease.

Anna continued to be amazed at the effect co-operation played in their community. It was awesome.

LATER THAT EVENING, after Jed and Lisa had gone to bed, Matt and Anna remained outside at their firepit. The nights were already becoming cooler, a sign that summer was losing its edge. Anna threw a blanket over both their knees for added warmth instead of adding more fuel to the fire.

"Shall we go in, sweetie?" Matt yawned and stretched his arms out, the day's labor catching up with him.

"Not yet. I think we've got a problem we should talk about."

"Sure. What's up?" Matt angled his chair towards her so that he could pay attention.

"Have you and Ray spelled out the rules for our boys regarding sex? They're both at that horny stage, where all girls look wonderful, and they're eager to experience what it's like to be in love."

"Well, of course, we've talked to Jed and Aaron. They know the drill and know we expect them to behave."

"Yes, but you remember what it was like for us at that age. You'd swear that you wouldn't cross the line, then the kissing starts, and the feelings mount up to a point where you can't stop. If you haven't given them condoms, I think you should think about it. Being a nurse, I've seen too many young teens giving birth before they're mature enough to be mothers."

"Somehow, I don't think that's something I'm comfortable with. After studying the Bible with our kids and letting them know what we believe about this subject, I don't want to be handing them condoms. It's almost like I'm permitting them to be promiscuous. I'm sure if Jed were heading that way, he'd look after that himself. Why, is there something going on that I'm not aware of?"

"I'm not sure. Both Kari and I have noticed some interesting body language between Jed and Chloe. It looks like they're resisting the temptation to be together, but virtuous intentions at that age are easily forgotten in the heat of the moment. I wouldn't want to see them go over the line and then deal with a pregnancy. That wouldn't be great for them, us parents, or our community. I should take Lisa and Chloe for a hike soon and share quality time. I could bring up what I've seen at the hospital and get into the dilemmas they will face as their bodies mature."

"Hmm. You better check with Denyse first. She may not like that someone else is talking to her daughter about sex." Matt rubbed the back of his neck as he pondered the right way to approach this. "Ray and I will talk to our boys separately and reinforce the rules. I'll make it clear that Chloe is off-limits. She's too young to get sexually involved. And if he wants to go to university, it's a lot easier when he's single than when he has a wife and baby beside him. Accidental pregnancies happen all the time, so if he can't stay celibate, he'll need to be responsible and get protection for himself and his girlfriend."

"There's no use turning a blind eye and hoping these

kids don't feel the pull of the opposite sex. It would be strange if they weren't experiencing it. Most teenagers think they can control the situation and aren't prepared when their libidos explode. You need to tell them to expect these emotions and know how to get out of temptation's way. At their age, teenagers are not thinking about the Ten Commandments."

"I guess so. When did they grow up? I thought we were years away from this." Matt closed his eyes, frowning at the newest problem.

"You know how the saying goes 'in a blink of an eye.' Look how much they've grown in the past six months. It was bound to happen. We'd like to have them stay beside us so we can protect them and guide them, but the time is quickly coming that they'll have to take responsibility for everything they do."

"I guess so. We've been lucky. We've hardly had any problems, and I was hoping it would continue that way."

"It probably will, but who knows? They've had a good upbringing within the Church, and now with this commu- nity. It's shaped them. I'm confident that even if they do slip, they'll reach out to us for advice." Anna patted her husband's hand, hoping to reassure him.

"I hope so, darling. It scares me to think otherwise. I guess when we join Thomas and Sonja on the fishing trip this weekend, I better carve out time to go over this."

"Good idea. You talk to Jed, and I'll talk to the girls. Make sure you emphasize that we'll always be there for them, no matter what. Until then, let's look up at the stars, give thanks, and pray. We've done everything we can. It'll be up to Him to watch over and guide our kids as they become independent." Anna reached for her husband's hand, and together they began the Lord's prayer.

CHAPTER 11 - ONE YEAR LATER

Denyse and Chloe were taping the last of the twirled mauve crepe paper down the long table the bride and groom would occupy with their parents.

"This is beautiful, Chloe. You've done a great job decorating the head table."

"Thanks, Mom. Lisa's almost finished decorating the gift and book signing table. After this, I'm going to help her and the ladies with the banquet table."

"I'm so proud of you girls. When you're finished with that, you should probably head home to get ready." Denyse's eyes watered as she thought about Pete. He would've been so pleased to see how well his family was coping. She knew that spiritually he was there with them, smiling. After the initial shock of their father's passing, the children had become protective of each other and their mother.

"I know, Mom. I sense Dad right here beside me too. Even Mike says sometimes he hears dad's voice, then he turns around, and of course, he's not there. But Mike swears that Dad's talking to him. Telling him to be brave."

"I don't doubt that if there's a way he could talk to us, he will find it. I believe his soul is staying close to us, making sure we're okay."

"Me too." Chloe's eyes misted as she went and hugged her mom. "We'll be okay, Mom. Whatever you want to do is fine with Mike and me." She stepped back as she heard Lisa call her name. "I'm coming!"

Chloe skipped towards the kitchen area, shouting back to her mom. "Gotta go. That girl has no patience. She'll keep screaming until I get over there."

Denyse pulled her fingers away from her cheek, where Chloe had kissed her soundly. It'd been a long time since her daughter had shown her so much affection. It felt good. She'd been Daddy's girl, yet here she was, making sure that her mom was coping.

When Thomas and Sonja had approached her after their engagement announcement at Christmas to perform their wedding ceremony, she had quickly agreed. She was proud that they had asked her to officiate. Being the considerate couple they were, they had called after Pete passed away, saying Sonja understood if she'd like to pass on their nuptials, that they could get the minister from her parent's United Church.

After several days of prayer and discussion with Chloe and Mike, she agreed that being part of their celebration would be good, affirming the continuity of life. Her family needed the joyous fellowship of their community more than ever before. After all, Sonja was expecting a baby in October. The reason for all seasons was life.

Denyse walked around the hall that would hold the reception. The bride and groom, along with their parents, would be sitting at the head table. Sonja's brother, Luke, and

Anna would join them as best man and matron of honor. Mrs. Hansen had brought her Royal Copenhagen Princess China for the head table to supply 'something borrowed, something blue.' Mrs. Kerr donated crystal wine glasses and the delicate lace tablecloth her mother had crocheted for her wedding. Two families sharing their heirlooms to bless Thomas and Sonja on their journey together.

A flurry of activity at the hall entrance caught everyone's attention. Ray and Matt had gone to pick up Jed and Sonja's best friend, Colleen, from the airport, as well as the rental tuxes for Luke and the boys. They were due to arrive from Vancouver yesterday, but high winds had forced a flight cancellation. Not unusual for this time of year.

"Denyse, come and meet Colleen before I bring her to our guest cabin. Everybody?" Matt yelled loudly to get their attention. "Come and meet Sonja's best friend. She almost chickened out after yesterday's windstorm, but she made it. Although when she saw the mountain peaks she was flying over, Colleen had to close her eyes and remind herself why she'd risked it."

Colleen blushed at the gentle teasing and seemed overwhelmed with all the hugs she received from strangers. Denyse took mercy on her and motioned for Matt to take her away so she could get settled and dressed for the ceremony that was only two hours away.

Denyse asked Mike to find Brianna and tell her that the hall would be ready for photos soon. Then she returned to the kitchen with her list, checking and crossing off the last-minute things.

Vera and Kari were busy making the final touch-ups on the arrangements of wildflowers that Chloe, Lisa, Mike, and Aaron had collected over the past few days. The kids were proud of the gift of alpine flowers they gathered for the wedding. Yellow mountain arnica entwined with purple Camas and white valerian adorned small vases on each table. The larger bouquets in the tall, wicker baskets on either side of the podium were composed of Magenta alpine fireweed mixed with Delphiniums and white daisies.

The bride and matron of honor would have small bouquets of delicate pink sea blush and wild bleeding hearts interspersed with sprigs of wild lavender.

Lisa and Chloe joined everyone in admiring the flowers, particularly amazed by the bride's bouquet.

"I never thought all those flowers would end up looking that good in a bouquet. That's the most beautiful arrangement I've ever seen." Lisa bent to sniff the fragrant blooms. "That's what I'll do someday. I'll be a florist and make people happy with my designs."

Chloe rolled her eyes.

"Don't you believe me?" Lisa asked.

"You're always changing your mind about what you want to do. It seems to me that your last career choice was to be a pilot. What happened to that idea?" Chloe elbowed her friend gently and grinned. Her eyebrows lifted as if expecting a denial.

Lisa elbowed Chloe back and stuck her tongue out at her. "Maybe I'll do both. I've read that most adults have four or five careers in their lifetime. Who knows how many I'll have?"

"Alright, girls, I think Gwen and Aunt Kari could use a hand in the kitchen. Then you should go home and get dressed. Showtime is in two hours." Denyse waved them to the kitchen. "I'll head home first and get ready. See you soon."

"Our first wedding. It's beautiful, isn't it?" Anna said to Kari as they walked through the hall, checking the details.

Two decorated long tables sat along the west wall, which Matt and Ray would move to the center floor after the ceremony. Salads, appetizers, and main course items would fill the tables for the smorgasbord dinner. Sonja had picked a two-tier wedding cake, which Kari had finished decorating yesterday. After dinner, she'd bring it out and place it on a side table where the bride and groom would later cut and serve it. There was also a selection of Mrs. Hansen's famed Norwegian desserts.

Including everyone from Safe Haven, Sonja, and Thomas' families and close friends, there would be close to sixty people attending. Thomas had arranged for a sound system operated by Sonja's brother, Luke. It would be their first dance and the first wedding held at Safe Haven, and Thomas wanted it to be a fun affair.

"You've done an amazing job, Kari. This celebration will be a wonderful memory for them during the years to come." Anna was proud of her sister's ability to organize and put out a spread like this.

"It wasn't just me. It took all of us to get this ready, but thanks for the compliment."

"Strange how life goes. A year ago, Sonja wasn't sure she'd ever want kids, let alone get married. Now, look how happy she is. I'm glad she and Thomas figured it out."

"What was the problem—did you ever find out?" Kari asked.

"Independence. She didn't want to be tied down. Sonja was scared if she stayed in Bella Coola, she'd never experience the thrill of exploring geological sites worldwide. When Thomas took her to Niagara Falls last summer, she realized her dreams could still happen."

"Good. It may not be the same as being a vagabond, traveling whenever she feels like it, but there are other things just as important to enjoy."

"I think Sonja sees that now. Thomas wants her to be happy. He'll make sure she carves out time from their lives to reach her goals."

"Where's Jed? I thought he was arriving on the same flight as Colleen's."

"He's probably touching base with Aaron. I'm happy that Thomas and Sonja agreed to a June wedding so that Jed could come home. I miss him. His dad misses him."

"We all do. I'm glad you and Matt decided to let him go on his own and start his studies in Vancouver without waiting for Aaron. I think he needed to be independent for the first time in his life. I'm betting he's gained a new appreciation for his parents and this community."

"I hope so. Jed has a good head on his shoulders, but he can be just as stubborn as I am. It was hard to argue against his viewpoint when I used the same reasons to stay behind in Olympia."

"True. And knowing that Matt followed his instincts to carve a new life while hiding it from his family must have also tempted him to insist on the right to his own decisions." Kari spread her hands out in front of her, tilting her head to one side. "The apple didn't fall far from the tree."

"I know, I know. I'm sure Jed's also realized there's a price to pay for that independence. He's never experienced loneliness before. I hope you're right about the impact that's had on him."

Following her heart back home, Anna hurried to see her son. Although she looked forward to their online visits, FaceTime didn't really cut it. Deep voices and teasing laughter carried across the field. She spied a group congregating on Kari's back porch, a reunion between her son and his best friend and cousin, Aaron. Ray and Matt were there also, sitting on the railing and drinking a beer as they watched their sons catch up with each other.

Anna headed towards them. "Hey, you!"

Jed jumped down the stairs and ran to hug his mom. "Hi, Mom." He hugged her fiercely, swaying back and forth. "I've missed these hugs. I never thought I'd admit it, but I've missed you and Dad. Even Lisa. Where is she, by the way?"

"Finishing up in the hall with Chloe. They should be returning soon to get ready for the ceremony." Anna eyed her son up and down. "You've grown another few inches, haven't you? You've lost weight too."

"I haven't lost weight at all. It just looks like it because I've gotten taller. I don't cook as well as you or Aunt Kari does. I eat a lot of frozen pizza and Kraft dinner."

"Oh Lord, I'll have to send you back with my easiest recipes, plus the spices to make them. You probably only have salt and pepper?"

"No, I've got garlic and Montreal Steak Spice, too. That stuff can make anything taste better." Jed laughed at his mom's raised eyebrows. "Don't worry, Mom. When I get tired of my cooking, I either go to the cafeteria or hook up with my friends. We pick up groceries, and the girlfriends help us make something edible."

"Girlfriends? When did that happen?" Aaron piped in.

"Bob and Tony have girlfriends, and I have a classmate that I see a lot, who's a girl—but not a girlfriend." Jed's face turned pink with the revelation, obviously expecting some inevitable needling.

"Right. Just a friend." Aaron leered. "What's her name?"

"Amanda. She's in my science and English Lit class. She lives in White Rock, not far from UBC. They were one of the contacts the Zanettis set up for me if I ever needed help. I have to pass on their condolences to the family for them."

"Yes, it's been a tough start to the New Year, losing Pete so quickly. There have been many changes in the year since you've been away. Good thing I've kept busy with telenursing, and your dad has his dental practice in Williams Lake. It's helped take our minds off missing you. Having this marriage to concentrate on has been a blessing. Mrs. Zanetti will perform the ceremony this afternoon." Anna said.

"How's Chloe and Mike doing? I've emailed her, but she doesn't say much."

"She's been a rock for her mom and Mike. Which surprised me because I thought she'd be the one to fall apart. Mike was with his dad when he collapsed. He called me, and I went over right away and performed CPR while we waited for the ambulance to get there. Denyse and Chloe were grocery shopping in town, and they arrived just before the paramedics. His last wishes were not to be put on life support, so when Denyse arrived, she made me stop resuscitating him. The EMTs placed him on their bed and let them have time with him before transporting him to the hospital."

Jed's eyes had begun to water as he listened to what Chloe and her family had gone through. "Yikes, that must've been tough."

"It was. Denyse told me that they knew the end was

coming. The last time he went to the hospital for a blood transfusion, they were very kind but told them it wouldn't help. The family had been preparing for this, talking and praying together. So, even though it wasn't a surprise, it was still an ending they didn't want."

Aaron shouldered his cousin. "I've taken Chloe and Mike ATVing quite often since then, just to get them away. Remember how bubbly and chatty she was all the time? Not so much now. Mike talks a lot. I think he enjoys escaping from the sadness around his house. I'm doing what I can to help."

Anna watched the interaction between the boys and noted the ambivalence that Jed tried hard not to show. The first year away from home was always the toughest. He was still deeply connected to Chloe and the rest of the family, indeed for the community as a whole. Even though their time at Safe Haven was relatively brief, it had made an impact on Jed. She glanced over to her husband and knew Matt was probably thinking the same thing. He was pleased that Jed missed the place.

"I'll offer to take her out tomorrow then if she's up to it. We've got lots to talk about. And I miss the freedom of heading into the hills any old time I want to. City life sucks sometimes."

"It'll be better next year when I get there. I have a knack for keeping things interesting."

"Probably. Have you decided on university or BCIT?

"It's still a toss-up. It kind of depends on my SAT scores. I love working with Dad. It's kind of neat knowing that what we build could last a hundred years or more. I'm debating whether to get my ticket for carpentry or apply to become an electrician. Or stretch myself and become an architect."

Aaron wagged his head from side to side as he weighed his possibilities.

"So, what else have you been up to without me?"

"Mark started building a cedar strip canoe just before Easter, a project he said he'd postponed forever. He asked me if I wanted to help him, and I jumped at the chance. We were only working on the project for a week when I asked him if I could make my own at the same time. He said sure if I was allowed, so we've been working on that since January." Aaron stood a little taller, his chest puffed out with pride. "There's a lot of sanding to do and steaming to curve the boards, but I'm really enjoying it."

"Cool. How come you never told me that? Can we take a look? Mom, have we got enough time?"

"Sure, but not more than an hour. We'll shower and dress first. Then you can be the last one to get ready." Anna patted her son on the shoulder, then kissed his cheek. "I'm so glad to have you back home."

Jed and Aaron bounced down the step and over to a covered area beside the maintenance building where the construction was happening.

Anna walked to stand beside Matt, wrapping her arm around his waist. "Feels good to have him here again." She contemplated her husband's quiet mood and saw that hungry look in his eyes.

He'd confided that he missed his son possibly even more than she did. Father and son had been so close in the last few years that Anna understood Matt sometimes felt he was missing a part of himself.

She understood that feeling well and hugged her husband tightly. "He'll be home for the summer now. You'll have lots of time to catch up."

At 4:30, all the families began to wander up to the main lodge to help in last-minute arrangements before seating themselves. Matt had met Thomas a half-hour prior, trying to calm him down from the wedding day jitters. Sonja would be arriving with her family at five o'clock. Once everyone was seated, and the bride and Anna were ready, Chloe would play the guitar, a rendition of Sonja's favorite song, *Breathe*. Sonja had found her soulmate and was excited to start their new life together.

Tyler and Troy arrived with their mom dressed in their rented Tuxes, their hair slicked down. Brianna was taking pictures of her sons on their best behavior. The two boys would be ring bearers for Sonja and Thomas. When they saw their Nana Gwen and Papa Mark, they tore across the hall, scrambling for hugs from them. Brianna took several shots of the happy foursome, deciding she'd frame one for the honorary grandparents. Then, she disappeared into a curtained-off area they were using as a staging area.

Anna was already there, trying to reach the clasp at the back of her neckline.

"Thank God. Can you do this for me? I'm so nervous that my hands are shaking."

"Sonja has great taste. You look beautiful in aubergine, and your bouquet is stunning next to it." Brianna checked her over, sliding her necklace slightly to the left to center the pearl pendant. The lavender and pink wildflowers were a perfect accent to her dress and would photograph well.

"Thanks." Anna peaked out of the curtain and saw the guests greeting each other and taking a seat facing the podium.

White wicker baskets of alpine wildflowers were on each

side of the podium, offering a romantic setting for the exchange of vows. Noticing Aaron and Jed enter with their freshly pressed suits made her heart swell with pride. They were heading to a row of seats that she could see was occupied by Lisa, Ray, and Kari.

Anna checked her watch and sucked in a breath of apprehension. 4:55, and the bride wasn't here yet.

Although it may be acceptable to be fashionably late, it also created heightened anticipation that prompted whispers in the audience.

Chloe sat beside the podium and strummed melodies to calm them. Her blonde hair had been pulled from her face and held by floral hairpins, then cascaded down her shoulders in soft waves. Her pale pink dress complimented her fair skin tones as it hinted at her maturing figure. Her rosy cheeks evidenced her nervousness despite the calm and demure expression, her eyes gazing downwards at her guitar.

Jed's back was ramrod straight as he listened to Chloe play, scrutinizing the changes since he last saw her. Aaron had elbowed him and whispered to his cousin, but Jed ignored him. When he followed the object of Jed's attention, he shrugged his shoulder and turned to speak to Lisa, but she was too busy fidgeting to pay attention. Rebuffed, Aaron sat quietly, watching the fuss this wedding had created.

Lisa had chosen a delicate yellow dress with a square neckline and flaring skirt and was smoothing it over her knees. She alternated to staring at Chloe playing the guitar and tugging at the hemline, probably regretting the length she had begged her mother to hem it.

It struck Anna how much her children had matured. It wouldn't be long that Aaron would join Jed in Vancouver. Only another few years and Lisa would be gone too.

At least for a while. Their children would go to university and broaden their horizons, but Anna and Matt hoped they would eventually return here. Time would tell. According to Matt, although problems had eased somewhat in Washington, it was still too challenging to resume their old life there.

Anna wondered if he'd ever be ready to give up the peaceful lifestyle he'd created here. Matt managed to balance his intellectual side and his Safe Haven, by setting up an endodontic practice in Williams Lake. He enjoyed resuming his skills in dentistry and worked one week per month. His reputation preceded him, and referrals kept his office booked for months in advance. Many small communities in the interior were happy they no longer had to travel to Vancouver or Prince George. Plus, it gave him a healthy cash flow to help maintain the intentional community he had designed.

His decision had influenced her into submitting her resume for telenursing through the BC Health Link services, and she also enjoyed using her skills again on a part-time basis.

Looking at her watch again, Anna sighed. 5:05. A flurry of activity from downstairs signaled that the bride and her parents had arrived.

SONJA SLID THE CURTAIN ASIDE, slipped in, and hugged Anna in excitement.

"Oh my. Your dress is gorgeous, and you look stunning," Anna gushed. "I love your shorty veil, very stylish."

Sonja had chosen the empire-waisted creamy colored

satin because it accented her skin tone and minimized her baby bump.

Anna kissed her on the cheek, then lifted her eyebrows. "I was beginning to worry how long Thomas was going to wait before going to look for you. He's been pacing for the past twenty minutes."

Sonja laughed. "Mom sent him a text and told him to hold his horses. We'd be arriving soon. Lucas had a wardrobe problem that Mom needed to repair. Renting tuxes doesn't guarantee a proper fit, as he soon found out when we started getting ready. You should have seen his face."

"So, everything is fixed? Are you ready to go? No second thoughts?"

"None. I can't believe I was scared of this. Thomas and I will have a beautiful life together. Having this baby to love and cherish will change my focus on travel for a while, but we're committed to having both in the future. I've never felt so centered before."

"I'm glad you two figured it out. Love wins. And if I have one piece of advice to give you, it's this. Marriage is a roller coaster. It has its ups and downs, but when you're committed to the love you have together, you work it out. Sometimes you compromise. Sharing your life gets a lot easier as time goes on. I know you'll both treasure every part of your marriage."

"Thanks, Anna. My mom and dad have been married for almost forty years. I hope we can enjoy it as much as they have." Sonja's vision began to mist. Stroking her fairly prominent baby bump made her even more teary-eyed.

Switching gears to save the makeup, Anna reached into the cooler and withdrew their bouquets. "Let's get this show on the road before both of us ends up sobbing." When Anna handed Sonja her flowers, they both paused to inhale the delicate scents now filling their makeshift bridal lounge.

"Hello in there? Can I take a few photos before you come out?" Brianna whispered loudly.

"Yes, of course." Sonja pulled the curtain aside, and Brianna entered.

"Alright. Anna take back Sonja's flowers, then I'll snap some shots of you handing them to her. And if you can check Sonja's hair and dress, that will make great souvenirs shots of your last minutes of single life." Brianna fussed with the lighting and angle then took several photos.

"Ok, it's showtime. When I leave, Gwen will bring the boys here with the ring boxes. I'll let Chloe know to start playing your song. Anna, you exit after the first few bars. You'll probably have to nudge the boys to get them started, but they know the drill. They've been practicing. Sonja, take fifteen or twenty seconds, breathe deep and get ready to start the next phase of your life. See you in a bit." Brianna leaned over and bussed Sonja on the cheek. "You're gorgeous. You're going to knock Thomas' socks off."

The three ladies giggled at that thought. Then they became reflective and nervously fiddled with their bouquets. Brianna left them, blowing them a kiss.

When the first note of 'Breathe' began, Anna poured them each a flute of sparkling water and toasted her friend. "To the love in your future. Be happy, my friend."

The girls clinked glasses and drank. Clearing her throat from emotion, Anna gave Sonja a little finger wave. "See you out there."

As the curtain fluttered shut, Sonja closed her eyes for a moment. Breathing deeply, she opened her eyes and took a step forward. Sonja parted the curtain and slowly emerged, beaming with anticipation, searching the sea of familiar faces for her forever love.

Thanks for reading *All for Family*. Want to know what happens next in the Taylor family saga? Keep reading for an excerpt from *All for Peace*.

DEAR READER

I hope you enjoyed reading Anna and Matt's story as much as I enjoyed writing it. If you did, please post a review online. Reviews are incredibly helpful to an author's success. They help readers find the books they love and motivate authors to keep writing those books.

You can review wherever you purchased *All for Family* and also on Goodreads and BookBub.

I love hearing from readers and plan to release more books soon. So visit my website www.LynnBoire.com, sign up for my newsletter, or email me at Lynn@LynnBoire.com to stay in touch and learn about my new releases.

An excerpt from *All for Peace* is on the next page.

Cheers,
Lynn Boire

ALL FOR PEACE - EXCERPT

~

CHAPTER 1

"No, I'm not going there!" Ellen refused to raise her eyes as she repeated herself. "I'm not seeing anyone. Tell him to—" She clenched her hands and lowered her voice to a growl. "Go. Away. Now."

"Alright, Mrs. Peterson, I'll ask your husband to leave. He's going to be very sad and hurt by your decision. You promised Dr. Hallden you'd see him today. He looked so excited to see you. Won't you at least give it a try?" Nurse Reid stooped to get to eye level with Ellen. When Ellen didn't respond, she sighed and shook her head, then retreated from the parlor. "I'm sure Dr. Hallden is going to be disappointed too."

Glad that the nurse hadn't forced the issue, Ellen barely noticed her leaving the room. She sat in her favorite chair in St. Joseph's Hospital's lounge area. She wasn't fully aware that she had won the battle, only that everything around her had closed in again, keeping her safe.

The walls were growing around her, and she wasn't going to let anyone in.

~

Purchase *All for Peace* and find out what happens next.

DEDICATION

I continue to be blessed with the loving support of my family and friends. They are the cornerstones in my life – Karen and Taylor, Brian, my husband Ron, and siblings Angie, Lorraine, and Irene. I genuinely appreciate my beta readers, Anne, Gina, Linda, Tricia, Darlene, and Dave, who offered their insights that helped me polish the Taylor family saga. I hope you enjoy it.

Keep reading to learn about all of the books in my *Safe Haven* series.

ACKNOWLEDGMENTS

I am very grateful for the Vancouver Island Romance Authors (VIRA) group in British Columbia, Canada. Their monthly meetings and workshops continue to inspire me. The authors have been generous with their advice and perceptive insights, a more supportive group would be hard to imagine. Jacqui Nelson continues to be the mentor I turn to, and she never disappoints. She is always prompt, integrity conscious, and intuitive about the direction I'm moving towards in my books. I appreciate her dedication beyond words.

ALSO BY LYNN BOIRE

THE SAFE HAVEN SERIES

All for Love

A Safe Haven Cli-Fi Suspense Novel

Obsession. Betrayal. Chaos.

Matt Taylor secretly builds a Safe Haven far from the chaos in Washington State. Will his dream for a secure and sustainable lifestyle be everything he hoped for?

All for Family

A Safe Haven Rediscovery Novel

Reunite. Respect. Restore.

After Anna Taylor honors her professional commitments to her community in Olympia, she finally joins her family in Bella Coola. Together they and five other families tackle the challenges of thriving and surviving in an intentional community.

All for Peace

A Safe Haven Self-Discovery Novel

Secrets. Murder. Insanity.

Matt's cousin, Ellen Peterson, avoids conflict at all costs to maintain her illusion of a peaceful and successful family.

But secrets can kill. Can Ellen live with that?

ABOUT THE AUTHOR

Lynn Boire enjoyed a successful career in dental office management, but it was never her passion. Always a voracious reader, she began a process of self-discovery in the '80s and realized creative writing was her passion and future.

Lynn writes contemporary suspense that reveals how women who avoid conflicts whenever possible in their relationships, find the confidence in themselves to voice their opinions. As they become more independent, they gain the inner strength to take control and enrich their lives.

Lynn lives in a seaside town on Vancouver Island in British Columbia, Canada. She uses her deep appreciation of every part of her island home for the background in her stories. She feels a spiritual connection whenever she's near a body of water. Nature puts everything in perspective, and all her doubts and worries float away. Even if a storm's strength frightens her, it also reminds her that—no matter what—all things pass. Lynn is blessed with many friends and family, including her husband, two grown children, a grandson and his daughter, and a stepdaughter and her family.

LynnBoire.com

amazon.com/author/lynnboire
goodreads.com/author/show/20765007.Lynn_Boire
bookbub.com/authors/lynn-boire
facebook.com/lynnboire

Manufactured by Amazon.ca
Bolton, ON

24950107R00125